THE CEO

NIQUEL

DEDICATION

This book is dedicated to my girls K1&K2. This book has taken a lot of time away from you and you still believe in me and tell me you love me every day! You are mommy's little rays of sunshine and make me strive harder to achieve my dreams! Love you!

I also dedicate this book to my Grandparents Mo & O. You mean the world to me and have taken care of me my entire life. Anything artistic I wanted to do, you backed me 100%. Thank you!

To the rest of my family, you've all been there to see my struggles and have pushed me to be the best I can be. Thank you and I love you all!!

I also dedicate this book to everyone who has told me to shut up and stop worrying, you know who you are! I finally believe you!

And to Chris, I know I've pissed you off the most, but you were the first to believe in this project. Thanks!

Lastly, to my readers old and new, thank you for your support!

CONTENTS

ACKNOWLEDGMENTS

I'd like to give a special shout out to my bad ass beta readers! You've seen this book before ANYONE. You told me what sucked, what worked, and have been honest with me the entire time. You've all stayed with me even though life got in the way and that's very rare. I'll never be able to repay you enough for it, but I really appreciate you very much!

To: Sydney H, Cindy W, Krystin G, Jenna S, Celena T, Samaris C, Aimee O, Carmen P, Amy W, Lorelei M, Sara F, Betty V, and Taryn B. I love each and every one of you ladies! Thanks for sticking with me and never giving up on me, you rock bad asses!

Shout out to Kim G for the last minute proofread!

Shout out to Tahseen for helping me be authentic!

To my biff Devon, thank you for talking me off the ledge!

PROLOGUE

I was born in a small town just outside the capital of Riyadh, Saudi Arabia. As a family of five, we struggled a lot to make ends meet. My father bounced from job to job, just to try to keep us afloat, and my mother stayed at home to care for me and my younger brother, Kieran. My older sister Shannon was of age already, so she was able to attend public school just across the road from our home. We weren't allowed to start school until we were six and I missed the cutoff date by several weeks.

We finally received some good news: Dad found a stable job as a delivery driver at a well-known bakery in town called Neerah's. Things were finally starting to pick up for our poor family, until the unthinkable happened: Mom got *sick*.

Dad tried his best to pick up as many hours as he could at the bakery, while my siblings and I tried our best to take care of Mom and keep her as comfortable as possible. We couldn't afford any traditional medicine for her, nor did we even have a formal diagnosis. This tore my father apart.

A month after her illness struck, she passed away and it devastated us all. Mom had been my rock, and always told me she believed I had the potential to be something great—*powerful* even.

Growing up, I never knew much about my other family members. Mom told us that her parents had passed away and Dad never told us anything about his parents. One night he came home and summoned us all to the living room. "My children, it is unfortunate that your mother is no longer with us, but I have some good news for you. We're going to the United States and we will live the American dream."

"How?" I asked.

"I know I've never mentioned him before, but your grandfather is a very wealthy man. He was digging in the mines of Egypt some years ago and struck oil with his friend, Rahmid. He's too old to maintain his company now and has entrusted me with a share of his oil business. Traveling to and from the States has become too stressful for him. With this money, none of you will ever have to work again, unless you choose to. But remember this: with great money comes great power, so don't let it define you—you need to define it."

I was only a child at the time, but I took everything he said to heart.

ONE

Boston, MA

Present day

"Do you need anything else, Ms. Quinn?" Karen said as she walked into my office with a mug full of coffee.

"No, that's it for today Karen. Just leave the coffee on my desk and you can take the rest of the afternoon off."

"Really? There are piles of paperwork to be sorted through, properly labeled, and filed."

"There's always tomorrow. Have a good day, Karen."

"Thank you, Ms. Quinn."

Karen was one of the first employees my father hired. She was honest, dedicated to the company, and always kept an eye on me when I used to visit as a child. My dad had a lot of trust in her and her judgment. She had black hair with silver strays mixed in, which she wore neatly pulled to the back of her head. She had olive skin and always wore a two-piece pant suit. For an older lady, she still looked amazing.

I'd been under a lot of stress recently. My dad's sixty-fifth birthday was fast approaching and he'd made the tough decision to hand over the company to his colleague Roger and myself. I was the only child of his that he could trust with such a huge responsibility and it was truly an honor. My older sister cared more about the latest looks in Hollywood and fashion trends, while my younger brother focused his attention on drugs and alcohol. Dad trusted Roger to an extent, but he wanted me around to make sure the company never lost its traditions or values.

I'd decided to plan a surprise party for Dad and wanted to give him nothing but the best. I ordered catering from his favorite restaurant, Ali's. They had the best roti and curry in town. The cake was coming from Kondito's Bakery, a shop he had gotten every single one of our birthday cakes from since we moved to Massachusetts years ago. The last thing on my list was to order fresh flowers from Skylar's Boutique and Rose Garden.

I locked the office up early and headed over to the boutique. This was something that had to be done in person and not arranged over the phone because everything had to be *perfect*. I pulled up in front of the boutique and noticed a tall male standing behind the counter through the glass. His hair was dark, short, unruly, and just long enough to run your fingers through. His back was facing toward me, and there was something oddly familiar about him, but I just couldn't put my finger on it. I shut the car door and as I approached the entrance, he turned around. *Shit, that's not—it can't be!*

I caught a glimpse of his face and instantly stopped in my tracks. I removed my hand from the door knob and slowly backed away from it, hoping he didn't spot me.

A flood of emotions took over and I made myself take a deep breath to calm the hell down. I wasn't the same Sheila Quinn he once knew. I was new and improved and didn't back down from anyone. Being weak was no longer my forte, or so I thought.

After my pounding heart settled in my chest, I grasped the handle and went inside. "Quinn? Sheila Quinn, is that you?" he said as he scanned my body from head to toe. I felt his gaze burning right through my pinstripe pencil skirt and blouse.

"Yes, Liam. It's me."

"How are you? How have you been?"

"I'm fine," I said without hesitation. "But I didn't come here for a walk down memory lane. I came here to order some flowers. Now if you can

4

help me with that and keep this as cordial as possible, then you'll still receive my business. If not, I'll go to Long's shop instead."

"Sure, I can do that. You look great by the way."

The man I'd almost married three years ago was standing right in front of me. Still sexy, still in shape; the only difference was that he seemed happier now. When we were together, he ran his own company named Castle Investments and was the number one man to beat in the stock exchange game. I stood by his side through all of his successes and *failures*. Eventually his company went down in flames for fraud and bad overseas investments. I had warned him that something didn't seem right about the foreign investors, but because I was on the outside looking in, my opinion didn't matter at the time.

He became so infuriated, so distraught over his losses that I couldn't bear to be around him anymore. He became a hostile drunk and completely drove a wedge between us. He was all I had, the only man I had ever let get close to me, and he tore my heart to shreds. After a year of neglect and emotional drainage, I finally got sick of his shit and called off our engagement.

He smiled at me and led me into the huge garden center. It was like a mini green house connected to the back of the store. Beautiful potted plants were hanging from the ceiling in neat, tight rows. Any kind of flower you could imagine was most likely labeled and had its own row in that room.

"What exactly are you looking for, Sheila?"

"Something beautiful and elegant that will last more than a day."

"So you're looking for something much like yourself. Let's see what we have, shall we?"

After choosing several different types of gorgeous exotic flowers, we went back to the front of the store to complete my order.

"Thank you for your help, Liam. Let me know when they're ready."

"I will. So Sheila, are you single?"

"Yes, why?"

"Just curious, I figured someone as beautiful as you would be married by now."

"Well you figured wrong." *And if you weren't such a jerk back then, I would be married right now.*

"Okay, well I'll talk to you later," he said with a mischievous grin.

A chill went down my spine as I exited the boutique. I had a feeling this wouldn't be our last encounter, but that didn't bother me because nothing was going to happen between us.

TWO

"Congratulations, Mr. Quinn! It has been such an honor and a privilege to work for you the past twenty years. You will truly be missed," said Rose.

"Thank you Rose," he said as we all raised our glasses to toast.

I hated Rose with a passion; she was such a kiss ass. She always tried to get special attention from my father but he never gave her the time of day. He was only interested in two things: his *business* and his *children*. Not some forty-year-old ex house wife. She actually had the audacity to wear a mini skirt and nude stockings today, showcasing her varicose veins to the entire room.

"Sheila, come over here for a moment. I need to speak with you," Dad commanded.

He took my hand and led me into his office. He had the biggest suite in the entire sixty-story building. Authentic Egyptian cotton curtains draped the windows, hand stitched Persian rugs decorated the floor, and the entire office was filled with black leather and pine furniture.

He told me to have a seat on his leather upholstered chair, and as I looked around the office, I envisioned it as my own.

"Sheila, this is all yours now. Decorate it how you want, but please try and get along with Roger—for me. Oh, and I know you don't like her much, but Rose and I are going out for dinner tomorrow."

"Seriously? Dad she's so desperate and—"

"Stop it, Sheila! You live your life, and I'll live mine. You know no one will ever replace your mom in my heart, but it's time I concentrate on other things now, like making myself truly happy. If Rose is a part of my journey, so be it."

"Okay, Dad," I sighed.

With the talk I'd had with my dad at the party the night before fresh in my mind the next morning, I walked around the office and decided it was in serious need of an update. It needed a feminine and professional look.

"Knock, knock."

"Yes, Rose?"

"If you need help redecorating, I know a great guy for the job."

"Thanks."

"Listen, Sheila. I know that you don't care much for me, but I want you to know I would never hurt your father. I have nothing but his best interest at heart."

"Okay," I said, trying my best not to roll my eyes at her.

I grabbed the card from the florist shop out of my desk and ordered two dozen flowers. I knew they wouldn't last long but they'd enhance the drab scenery.

As I sat at my desk filling out the annual drilling and construction form to verify our sites were up to date, Karen informed me that the flowers had arrived.

"Thank you, send them in."

Liam walked through the door with two huge glass vases and four dozen flowers. I was completely caught off guard and tried to maintain my composure. "I only ordered two dozen."

"I know. The rest are on me. Purple orchids are still your favorite, right?"

I felt a slight heat in my cheeks. "Yes."

"I thought so. Now where would you like me to put these?"

"Anywhere you'd like." I watched as he set the glass vases down on each end table. His white shirt clung tightly to his torso as he removed the protective plastic from the bouquets and snipped the ends with a pair of scissors.

"Like what you see?" he said with a smile.

"Maybe," I said as I felt a small pulse under my skirt.

He removed his gloves and walked over to me with his gray eyes fixated on mine the entire time. I moved to the edge of the desk and sat with my legs crossed before he approached me. He lowered his lips to my ear and whispered, "Is there anything else I can do for you?"

"No, that'll be all for now. If I need more flowers, I won't hesitate to ask."

He laid his hand on top of my thigh, gently hiking my skirt and exposing more of my flesh. "You know what I meant, Sheila."

I wasn't used to this type of aggressiveness from him, but it kind of turned me on. I lifted my hand toward his chin and stood on my tiptoes. Placing my hand firmly around his neck, I whispered, "I'll be in touch," and let go. He smiled, grabbed his tools, and headed for the door, glancing over his shoulder at me once more before leaving my office.

There was a spark in his eye, something new, something exciting— something I'd never seen before. This wasn't the same guy I'd been engaged to, and I wanted to get to know the new version.

THREE

I always tried to keep my business life and personal life separate. At twenty-seven years old, it was no secret that I was addicted to sex. I loved the things men did to my body. Teasing it, torturing it, ruling it—but I never let them take control unless I wanted them to.

Tonight would be one of those nights: a night I'd try to lose control. I was on my way to meet Rick, a twenty-three year-old model from Singlematch.com. Ten to one it wasn't really him in his profile picture, but as long as the guy looked decent and had a functional cock, I could work with it.

We agreed to meet at a hotel of his choice. It was very fancy and definitely exceeded my expectations. The lobby itself was two-stories high. A huge gold encrusted chandelier hung from the ceiling above the check-in counter and a maroon and a gold diamond patterned rug stretched from the entrance to a row of plush gold lounge chairs. I sat down on one of the plush lounge chairs and waited to hear from him. Not soon after my arrival, my phone beeped with an email notification.

FROM: BILLIONAIREMATCHMAKER

IF YOU'RE IN THE LOBBY, GO TO THE COUNTER AND LET THEM KNOW YOU'RE HERE TO SEE DICK CUNNINGHAM.

Dick Cunningham? Of Tech Corp? Shit. Tech Corp was a billion dollar software company that had originated in the Netherlands before making its way to the States after being bought out by Micromanagement Tech. He was a former business associate of my dad's and I knew I had to act fast or I was fucked.

I approached the desk. The receptionist handed me a gold key and told me to head up to the tenth floor where his private suite was located. I hadn't seen him in years and hoped he didn't recognize me.

Before entering the room, I slid my black masquerade mask out of my purse and placed it over my eyes. I brought it with me in the event I'd be put into a weird predicament where I didn't want to be recognized.

"Hello sweetheart. Sorry we had to meet under false pretenses, but I didn't want word to get out that the head of Tech Corp was cheating on his wife with online strays."

I politely smiled and nodded my head in understanding.

"Come here and let me get a good look at you," he said extending his hand from the king size bed.

Dick was your typical mid-forties businessman: well groomed, salt and pepper hair neatly tucked behind his ear, blue eyes, dark stubble, and a heavy set figure. I placed my purse down on the table and took a quick look around to check for weapons and map out an escape plan just in case things went haywire.

I stood in front of him with my dark locks pulled back into a neat bun behind my head, a black leather mini skirt, and a white blouse. He slid his sweaty hand up my thigh and gave my ass a tight squeeze. The material of my clothing bunched together between his fingers as he used his free hand to unzip my skirt.

"Why do you wear a mask?"

"Why do you pose as a twenty-something-year- old model, just for a piece of ass?"

He was taken aback at how sharp my tongue was, but I could tell it turned him on more than anything. I removed my shirt and stood in front of him with my purple lingerie set on. Grabbing my waist and pulling me closer to him, he slid one finger underneath the seam of my panties.

"You're very wet baby girl."

"Well, it's not every day I get to fuck a corporate big wig. Now take the rest of your clothes off and lay back," I demanded.

I hit the lights because I didn't want to see the disgusting face he'd make when he came, which judging by his size, would be in less than ten minutes. I tried my best to pretend he actually *was* the young model I'd seen in the picture just so I could get through it.

I climbed on his face and positioned my slit directly over his lips. I had no idea how bad of a fuck he was, but I knew I could teach him how to correctly eat a pussy.

After a pathetic attempt at sex, he rolled over and passed out soon after he released, which gave me an easy escape. I slid my clothes back on and walked out the door.

Never again! Next time, I'll make them show me some identification before I agree to meet.

I arrived at my condo and immediately ran into the bathroom to start the shower. I needed to wash the stench of disappointment off my skin.

Looking into the mirror, I realized I still had my black mask on. I peeled it off my face and admired my reflection for the moment: thick, full lips with red lipstick applied to them, hazel eyes, and my dark bun, still intact.

As the steam started fogging up the room, I hit the fan and pulled back the curtains, allowing the steam to escape. Then I slid my clothing to the floor and stepped inside.

The hot water relaxed and soothed my tight aching muscles, and washed away all the guilt I was holding on to.

FOUR

"Ms. Quinn, when would you like to start interviewing new interns for the company? You know your father always believed in helping the little man and I hope you will do the same."

"Of course I will Karen, why the hell wouldn't I?"

"I just thought—"

"Well you thought wrong," I interrupted. "Have you even started spreading the word about the vacant position yet?"

"Yes."

"Good, I'll check the website tomorrow for new applicants."

Karen knew I couldn't stand the way she down talked me. She still treated me like the little girl I once was. Brushing my annoyance off, I spun around in my leather chair and looked out the window. As I began to people watch, I saw the flower shop Liam worked at a few blocks away and reminisced about what had almost happened the other day.

Suddenly my phone rang, interrupting my gaze.

"Hello. Quinn National, Sheila speaking."

"Hi, my name is Grace Shieldman. I saw your intern posting online and wanted to set up an interview."

"Okay Grace, let me transfer you to Karen, she'll work out all the details. See you soon and good luck."

Most CEOs don't answer their own phone calls, but I had watched my dad personally answer all of his. He said it helped him feel more connected to his clients. He would also stay late and help out around the office because he genuinely cared about all of his employees like they were family.

This business was everything to him, and he knew he could trust me to keep it going.

After ten hours in the office, it was finally time to head home. I locked the door and took the elevator down to the garage.

There were two cars left in the lot besides mine and that struck me as peculiar. Usually this late at night, my black BMW was the only one left. I disabled my alarm and opened the back door to toss my briefcase on the seat. Before I was able to fully shut the door, a body pressed up against me and slammed me into it.

"Keep quiet and only speak when spoken to, got it bitch?"

"Yes."

"Now, what's a pretty thing like you doing here all alone?"

"I just got off work; why else would I be in a corporate parking spot this late?" I snarled at him.

My attacker spun me around and slammed my back up against the car. "Wrong answer. Do you want to die tonight?" he growled at me.

I made sure not to respond that time. I just tried to work out where I'd heard my attacker's voice before. He was over six feet tall with a husky build and a deep raspy tone to his voice. A black ski mask was covering most of his face so I couldn't properly identify him.

He placed his hand around my throat and slammed my back against the car once more. "I wonder what's hiding underneath that pretty pinstripe skirt of yours."

"I wouldn't do that, if I were you."

"Shut up," he yelled as his hand made contact with my face.

He kicked my legs apart while grasping my neck firmly. Pinning his body against mine to hold me in place, he took his free hand and ran his fingers up my thigh, then under the seam of my panties.

"Please don't."

"What's wrong sugar? You scared I'll hurt that tight corporate pussy of yours?"

I knew I had to act fast if I wanted to escape with my life. "Kiss me."

"What?"

"Kiss, me," I said, hoping he'd fall for my trick. As soon as his lips touched mine, I could grab his head, slam my forehead against the bridge of his nose, and run for it.

He placed his disgusting lips against mine and I thought my plan would work out smoothly, but it didn't. "You stupid bitch, you broke my nose!" He grabbed the back of my shirt, knocked me on the ground, and clasped both of his hands around my throat. I tried to kick him in the balls but he was too strong for me to overpower. Everything was starting to fade to black and in one last desperate attempt I reached for the rock underneath my car. I purposely left it there every day, as protection in the event tragedy ever struck. I grabbed for it and hit him on the side of the face, but that didn't work either. His grip on my throat tightened even more. I was fading, but before I slipped completely unconscious, I heard a familiar voice yelling my name.

I awoke in the hospital, bruised and battered, but otherwise okay. I didn't see any blood underneath my gown, which was a good sign. I reached between my legs and everything felt untouched. I paged the nurse so I could get some answers.

"Yes, Ms. Quinn? Is everything all right?"

"I'm not sure. How long have I been here?"

"Two days."

"Two days? What the hell happened to me?"

"You were physically assaulted in the parking garage at your office."

"Did anyone catch the asshole that attacked me?"

"No, but from what the witness described, the man seemed like he was out for blood."

"Do you know who the witness was?"

"He didn't leave a name, but he did deliver those purple orchids beside you."

"Liam..."

FIVE

A week had passed since my attack and everyone remained on high alert around me. I now had round the clock security guards patrolling the garage and waiting by the elevator when I exited the building. The cops occasionally popped in too, since my dad and the police chief were old friends.

My attacker was caught and identified as Raymond George, a former janitor that my father had fired the year before for stealing. He must have heard Dad had retired and decided to exact his revenge on me. Not many people knew about the elevator exit because it was in the back of the garage, in a secluded area.

"Sorry to interrupt Ms. Quinn, but your second interviewee is here."

"Send them in Karen."

A young man walked through my door. Tall, slender framed, with the bluest eyes I'd ever seen. His face was clean-shaven and his chocolate brown hair was slicked back and tapered on the sides. He carried a large briefcase in his hands. He extended his hand out, and I placed my hand in his. He had a nice, firm handshake and I could tell he meant business.

"Have a seat. So what is your name?"

"Ryan Smith."

"Where are you from, Ryan?"

"Montana."

"How old are you?"

"Twenty-two, ma'am."

"Why should I hire *you* as my intern?"

"Because I'm tech savvy, so I can update all of your outdated computer software. I'm a human number cruncher, and I can make a mean cup of coffee—or tea, whichever you prefer."

I admired the brass of this kid and decided to test him.

"Quick, what is two thousand five hundred and sixty-nine times three?

"Seven thousand seven hundred and seven. Come on now, are you serious?"

"Oh you're good. Be here at eight a.m. sharp tomorrow. Before you go, I want to make one thing clear."

"Yes."

"I want you to remember something: I am not your friend, I am not your mentor, I am your boss, and don't you ever think otherwise."

"I won't."

"Have a good day."

He picked up his briefcase and as he turned around I caught a glimpse of his slacks grasping his tight ass. I knew having him around would get me into trouble, but he was cute and it was a nice change from all the old hags walking around there.

SIX

"Good morning Ryan. I like my coffee with one sugar, light cream, and two scoops of hot chocolate mixed in. Think you can handle that?"

"I could make that in my sleep."

He promptly returned with the hot coffee and sat it down on my desk. I caught a whiff of his cologne on the way over and it was a sweet, musky scent.

"Thank you. Karen will give you your next assignment."

He walked out of the room with a huge smile on his face. *I hope the little jerk didn't spit in my drink.*

I turned on my laptop to check our stocks for the week and was interrupted by a phone call. "Hello. Quinn National, Sheila speaking."

"Go out with me."

"Who is this?"

"You know who it is, Quinn. I'd like to take you out for a date tonight. Nowhere fancy, just a nice place to eat and catch up, so to speak."

"Fine, Liam, you can pick me up after work at six."

That day in my office frequently crossed my mind. Liam was so aggressive, and it was such a huge turn on for me. I wasn't sure what tonight was going to be like, but I was positive it would end with us in between the sheets.

"Sheila, I know this may seem weird, but I really would like to try and work things out between us."

"Liam, I can't. I have a job to focus on now. I'm not that young intern that was so desperate for love anymore. Besides, it's been years; why do you suddenly want me back *now*?"

"I've never stopped wanting you Sheila Quinn. I was too stupid then to realize what I had right in front of me. We all make mistakes, and my biggest mistake was letting you walk out the door."

I could see the hurt in his eyes as he admitted that painful truth. I honestly never thought he cared, seeing as he started treating me like complete shit when his company went under. He never physically hurt me, but his absence and his distance took a serious toll on me. He was all I had besides my family. I'd made a vow that night to never depend on the love of another person *ever* again.

After dinner, he drove me back to my office's parking garage to pick up my car. "Thank you for the meal, it was nice."

"Sheila, I want you to come over tonight."

Part of me wanted to say no, but then I looked at him in that suit and knew I couldn't refuse his offer. Love or not, I was still highly attracted to him.

A short drive later, we arrived outside of a beautiful condo at the end of a private street. I opted to park on the street instead of in his garage so that I could easily run if needed. We walked up the front steps and once he opened the door, I was shocked at the view inside.

The wooden floors were so clean, glossy, and scratch free. He had a small island in the middle of his kitchen with two black bar stools in front of it. The living area was to the right, decorated with a black leather sectional, thin mirrors on the wall behind it, a faux tree, and black and white lamps beside it.

"Liam, your place is beautiful. How can you afford this working at a flower shop?"

"I didn't piss away all of my money you know. Besides, I'm co-owner of the boutique and business has been booming for months."

"Good for you."

"Would you like a glass of wine?" he asked.

"Sure, white Moscato if you have any."

"Of course, it's all I drink."

"Since when? You never liked drinking it before."

"Well, maybe I decided to branch out and try different things. Is that such a bad thing?"

"No, it's not."

He grabbed two huge wine glasses from the cabinet and opened the refrigerator door to pull out a large bottle of wine. Tilting the glass to the side, he slowly poured the chilled drink into one glass, then the other. Handing me one of the glasses, we clinked them together and said a quick cheers.

The wine was very smooth and had a faint citrus taste to it. "That was delicious," I said, placing the stem back on the counter.

"Glad you enjoyed it." He slowly walked over to me and opened his arms to hug me. As he wrapped them around my body, I placed my head against his chest and it almost felt like home. I quickly pulled back and freed myself from his grasp. "Sheila, what's wrong?" he asked.

"Nothing, I just—"

Before I could say another word his lips crashed upon mine. He yanked my hair free from my ponytail and placed a soft trail of kisses from my ear down the side of my neck. I wrapped my arms around his head, holding him there for a moment longer, embracing his familiar touch. I unbuttoned his suit jacket and peeled it off of his shoulders as he reached behind me and unzipped my dress, letting it fall to the ground. I pulled his arm and led him over to the couch, pushing him onto the leather material. If we were going to do this, I was going to be in control—*not him.*

SEVEN

"Sheila?"

"Yes?"

"Do you still love me?"

"Liam, not now, I'm trying to sleep."

I felt like I owed him a huge debt for saving my life that night. If he hadn't shown up when he did, there was no telling what would have happened to me. Maybe he'd been stalking me or maybe it was fate that brought him to the area; I wasn't sure, and I didn't care to find out—*yet*.

I rolled over, clutching the white sheet to my chest as we made eye contact. His eyes—his sweet gray eyes—always had the power to draw me in. His gaze pierced through my deepest layers, exposing my once fragile soul. I felt myself getting lost in him as feelings of love and joy from our past started to resurface. I had to try and snap myself out of it.

Ripping the covers off my body, I bent over and retrieved my outfit from the floor in a hurry.

"Sheila, what's wrong?"

"I—I have to go. I have an important meeting in the morning and I can't stay here fucking around with you all night."

"We weren't *fucking* around. You felt it too didn't you? I could see it in your eyes. You're just trying to deny the inevitable. We belong together, can't you see that?"

"No, it's nice to have sex with you once in a while, but we do not *belong* together."

"Quinn, I know you. All of you, inside and out, don't fight it."

I zipped my dress and slid my shoes over the heels of my feet, trying to ignore his comments.

"Bye, Liam," I said as I rushed out the door.

That was a close one Sheila. You've got to get your head back in the game!

I awoke the next morning, laughing at the thought of Liam and I back together. The sex was good—great even, but that's all I wanted. Maybe I was slightly delirious from having my head slammed against the concrete multiple times last week, but I knew what was best for me: just sex.

Arriving at my office an hour earlier than usual, I found Ryan in the conference room alone.

"Good morning."

"Morning."

"You're here awfully early, Ryan."

"I know, I was brewing a fresh pot of coffee and finishing up some last minute homework assignments."

"What are you in school for again?"

"Business."

"Good choice. Well if you ever have any questions, feel free to ask."

"I will. Thank you Ms. Quinn!"

I set my briefcase down and took my seat behind my desk. Ryan looked more attractive than I'd realized before. Something about him being in a normal button up shirt and jeans made him more appealing then the stuffy suit look. His hair was different too; it was gelled up into a little flip in the front of his head, making him actually look his age.

Tomorrow was the annual 'Save the Last Dance' event that my father had created five years before. It was made to welcome new employees to the company and make sure we could all get along in the same space. My father treated everyone like family and I'd promised to keep the tradition going.

"Here's your coffee, Ms. Quinn."

"Thank you. Hey Ryan, what are you doing tomorrow evening?"

"I have no idea."

"Good, you can be my date for the dance then."

The biggest grin formed on his face. I wasn't sure which D word made him happier, but I knew things could get very interesting.

Barely able to speak he muttered, "I—uh—yeah, count me in!"

"Good. Meet me here around seven so I can prep you. Since you're the newest employee here, you will be put in the hot seat *a lot*."

"That's okay, I can take it."

"Great, you'll fit in just fine here. Oh and Ryan? I hope to see you in proper work attire within the next ten minutes."

EIGHT

"Ms. Quinn, you look absolutely stunning tonight."

"Tonight Ryan, you can call me Sheila."

"Well *Sheila,* you're gorgeous."

"You're not looking too bad yourself."

I was wearing my black off the shoulder dress that stopped mid thigh and made my legs look exquisite. Accompanied by my black heels, lucky gold bracelet, hoop earrings, and loose side ponytail, I knew I was a force to be reckoned with. I had also applied my favorite bright red lipstick just before I met up with him.

Ryan was wearing a nice pair of black slacks with a blue button up shirt and a striped blue and black tie. He opened his arm to receive mine and we walked through the double doors together.

A loud roar of applause and whistles filled the air as soon as we walked through the entrance door. I was used to being in the lime light but poor Ryan was a bit on edge. I could tell he'd never been to a huge social gathering such as this before.

The hall was decorated beautifully. White drapery lined the ceiling with huge crystal chandeliers hanging from the center. Blue and white florescent lights illuminated the dance floor and round tables with crisp white tablecloths surrounded it. Huge flower centerpieces were set on each table with crystal gems hanging from each of them.

Rosa, the event coordinator, walked over to greet us. Her black hair and gray roots were a little frayed, but she still looked elegant in her white and black uniform. The light reflected off of her glasses as she pointed around the room, admiring her hard work. Her creations never ceased to amaze me.

"Rosa, you've really outdone yourself."

"Many thanks, Ms. Quinn. Is this your new boy toy?" she said, eyeing Ryan.

"Not yet," I laughed, nudging and winking at Ryan.

"Well, have a good night Ms. Quinn. My job is done."

"Night. See you at the next event."

I led Ryan to the head table where my dad and his big wig friends sat. It was the largest table in the room, covered in a bright blue tablecloth and decorated with silver and white flowers. My dad wasn't in to the over the top crystals and sparkles on the head table, so Rosa always omitted them.

"Sheila, should I sit here? I feel slightly out of place."

"Listen, you are my date and you'll be taken care of all night. You have nothing to worry about."

Stanley the waiter came over with four shot glasses full of whiskey. He knew how much anxiety I got from these stupid events and that these would help loosen me right up.

"What are these?" Ryan asked.

"Do you trust me?" I said, searching his eyes for the correct response. He nodded his head and we both chugged back the shots. The amber liquid burned my throat on the way down, but it was nothing compared to the pain of smiling and faking it for the people there.

I walked around the table and shook hands with everyone, with Ryan right by my side. He seemed to adapt pretty well to his new surroundings.

After hours of dancing, interviews, and socializing, it was finally time to leave. I had pounded back a ton of alcohol and it was finally starting to catch up with me. I tripped and fell into Ryan's arms as we were about to exit the dance floor. "Are you okay Ms. Sheila?"

"Sure, I drive now. Where is keys?" I slurred.

"Ms. Quinn, you cannot drive in this condition. We can go to my place down the street until you sober up and then I'll *think* about letting you leave."

Ryan left his car in the garage and took mine instead. My head was pounding and the sudden urge to vomit struck before he could stop the car in time, so I lurched out the window. "Sorry."

I awoke the next morning, completely clueless as to where I was or what exactly had happened the night before. My surroundings were unfamiliar and whoever the place belonged to had left me in his bed—alone. *Dammit Sheila, what random guy did you drunk fuck this time?*

The door opened and Ryan appeared in front of me with a mug filled with what I had hoped was hot coffee and handed me two aspirins. "Thanks. We didn't do anything, right?"

"No, but if I wanted to take advantage of you Ms. Quinn, I'd prefer that you were sober while I did it."

"Good," I said flashing him a slight grin. I took the coffee mug from him and took a small sip of the warm liquid to wash down the pills. I couldn't say that I was surprised I'd ended up there, but I was glad nothing had happened while I wasn't coherent enough to dominate him like he deserved.

He turned around, walked out of the room in his basketball shorts, and left me alone. Luckily it was Friday morning and Dad believed hard workers should never work on a Friday, Saturday, or Sunday; I never disagreed with that.

Before I could focus my attention on my escape plan, Ryan returned with a burrito in his hands. "What's in this?"

"Egg whites, cheese, peppers, onions, and turkey bacon."

"Good, pork isn't really my thing."

"I figured. You didn't strike me as the hog eating type."

"What in the hell is that supposed to mean?"

"Well, judging by your body, I can tell you love to keep yourself in shape, and any idiot should realize that. I'd rather be safe than sorry."

"You're right." I couldn't argue with that; I usually ran ten miles on the weekend, weather permitting. These legs didn't get so sexy on their own. I took my health very seriously, excluding the heavy drinking I occasionally indulged in.

NINE

It was the day I dreaded: the day I had to present my newest idea to the board of directors. Although our company wasn't struggling financially due to the high demand for oil, I wanted to add a more earth friendly alternative. I wanted to talk to them about converting some of our oil into natural gas.

"Sheila, the board is ready to see you now," Karen said.

My palms started to sweat, my stomach felt uneasy, and I could feel the beat of my heart in my throat. Most of those guys were scum bags and I knew if my words didn't persuade them, my body could.

I hiked my skirt up and unbuttoned the top clasp of my blouse. *It's time to eat these assholes alive.*

I clicked my heels into the conference room and set up my presentation board. The room was filled with a desperate circle of sex-deprived men. None of them took their eyes off me, not even the ones with shiny wedding bands wrapped around their ring fingers.

"Gentleman, as you may know, natural gas is economically convenient and a lot cleaner than heating oil, making it much better for the environment. Also, it currently costs less than heating oil and customers who chose to convert to this method of heating avoid high maintenance and equipment costs. There will be no need for pumps, motors, filters, or any type of special permits."

"And how much would it cost to convert?" one of the big wigs asked.

"Roughly between one and five thousand dollars. It really depends on the size of the current tanks they have, how old they are, and the details of the person's home we'll be entering."

"How will this gas get into their homes?"

"It'll be piped directly in their home from our distribution and service lines, which will be connected right to their meters."

"Do you really think people will go for this?"

"Yes, especially our elderly customers. They'll sign up for pretty much anything that sounds like it will save them a dollar or two."

"We like the way you think Sheila."

"Thank you sir."

"No, thank you."

"We just need a few moments to deliberate, and you'll have your answer soon."

"Thank you for your time and consideration." I packed up my boards and exited the room with a huge smile on my face. I could smell victory in the air and nothing could bring me down from that high.

On my way back to my office the head of the division—aka the man that decided yay or nay on my proposition—ran after me. "Sheila, wait."

"Yes, Reginald?"

"That was a fantastic presentation you gave back there, but I think I need a little more *convincing*, if you know what I mean."

I pushed him into the vacant conference room behind us and locked the door. Shoving him up against the wall, I placed my lips close to his ear, inhaling his sweaty white rain scent. "What kind of *convincing* do you need, Reg?"

He cupped my ass with his hands, slightly lifting me off of my feet, and ran his nose against my cleavage. "God, you smell amazing."

I wanted to let him *think* he was getting something from me, but there was no way in hell I'd fuck that sleaze ball. Once he placed my feet back on the ground, I grabbed a handful of his testicles. Grasping them as tight as I possibly could, I also bit the side of his neck for good measure. The stunned look on his face was priceless, and I think he got the hint.

"Yo-you can proceed with the natural gas project," he cried out after falling to the floor in agony.

"Thank you, and next time you might want to think about who you're dealing with. I'm not Amber, the company slut. With your salary, you couldn't afford to lick the bottom of my heels. So fuck you, and good day, sir!"

I opened the door and peered down the corridor to make sure no one saw me leave the room. The old hags had enough shit to say about me behind my back on a daily basis. I didn't want to fill their daily quota all at once.

Before I reached my office, I heard Ryan yell from the conference room, "So how'd it go?" I stopped in the doorway and smiled. "I have a good feeling natural gas is coming to Quinn National."

"That's fantastic, let's go out and celebrate tonight!"

"Shots on you?" I asked.

"Shots on me," he said with a one-sided grin.

I brushed my hair into a nice low bun at the back of my head and slid on my blue chiffon dress. It was light and flowy, perfect for a warm summer evening.

I felt uneasy about giving Ryan my home address, so I agreed to meet him at his place, and then he could drive from there.

He was sitting on his front steps awaiting my arrival. "Park your car here, we're traveling on foot tonight," he said through the car window.

"Good thing I decided to wear my flats tonight or I'd be screwed."
Sheila Quinn+ heels+ alcohol is *not a* good mix. "So, where to?"

"For you Ms. Quinn, we're going to the Watering Hole on Broadway."

"What the hell is that?"

"Only the best bar and grill in town. They make the best drinks and
their food is absolutely mouth watering. Trust me, you'll enjoy yourself.
Live a little, Sheila."

"Fine, let's go."

He didn't actually make us walk—thank goodness. He hailed us a cab
and we hit the downtown district.

We soon arrived in front of a first floor brick building with bright neon
lit signs in the windows. He opened the door for me, and surprisingly it was
very clean inside. There were wooden booths in the back, square tables and
chairs closest to the door, and a bar running from the kitchen alongside the
entrance.

The blonde hostess grabbed two menus and gave us a booth in the
back of the establishment. "Becky will be your waitress, she'll be with you
momentarily."

"Thanks," Ryan said.

A cute brunette quickly approached us and introduced herself. "My
name is Becky and I'll be taking care of you tonight. Would you like to start
off with some drinks?"

"Yes, four shots of whiskey please."

"You two must have come to party tonight. I'll be right back with
those."

"Might as well start the celebration off with a bang, right?" he said.

"Right," I agreed.

Several hours passed, and we were both drunk and exhausted from dancing all night. I felt like a normal person for once and not like Mr. Quinn's billion dollar princess.

"One more shot!" I slurred.

"Give her one more shot!" the crowd chanted.

I chugged back the last fireball and it packed a serious punch, almost knocking me to the floor. Luckily Ryan was there to catch me. "All right everyone, I think Sheila has had enough for tonight."

"Boo! Let her have one more shot, on me!" some random guy in the front yelled out. The bartender fixed one more fireball and I knew I had hit my limit.

Dizzy and stumbling out of the bar, Ryan couldn't help but laugh at me. "Wh-what?"

"You."

"Me, what?"

"For someone so small you drink enough to put any grown man to shame."

"I have an iron stomach," I said, slapping my abs. "Where to?"

"Back to my place."

A short cab right later, we were back at his place. I was still highly intoxicated and he was still slightly buzzed.

"Here, have a seat and I'll grab you some water and ibuprofen."

I tried to look around his apartment, but my head was pounding and the room was slightly spinning. I plopped down on the brown leather couch, which felt quite soft. He came back in, handing me the pills and a bottle of water. "Thanks."

I loosened my bun and let my curls fall free down my shoulders, then took the medicine. I placed the bottle on the coffee table and looked over at Ryan on the love seat. He was looking at me weirdly, almost creepily actually.

"What?"

"You should wear your hair down like that all the time. It makes you look so—so fucking sexy," he said as he moved from the love seat to my side.

He leaned forward, causing me to fall back on the couch, and slid his finger up and down the inside of my thighs. Positioning himself in between them, he leaned over to place a kiss on my lips, but didn't. "Not yet," he whispered in front of them. He climbed off of me and placed the blanket that had been draped across the back of the couch on me. I was so confused but too tired to think then.

TEN

The night had been insane, but also one of the best times I'd had in a while. Ryan was awesome to be around and I could really let my hair down with him. The sexual tension building between us was thick and although I didn't usually fraternize with my interns, he was the exception.

"Here's your coffee, just the way you like it Ms. Quinn. How are you feeling by the way?"

"I'm still a bit hungover."

"Once you're done with this cup, I'll gladly bring you as many as you need."

"Thanks." I realized the more Ryan and I hung out, the more he grew on me. He was quickly turning into my wing man and I felt I had nothing to worry about.

I received official word later that day that the natural gas division would be starting the next week and it was all mine. I was in charge of creating a logo, researching and mapping out what cities would benefit from the conversion the most, and also choosing the name.

The phone rang, disturbing me mid thought. "Hello. Quinn National, She—"

"Eila, I need you!" Before I could finish my greeting, I was interrupted by a familiar voice.

"Kieran? What's wrong?" My younger brother Kieran has called me Eila all of his life. When he was younger, he was unable to say Sheila, so I adopted the nick name and had it ever since.

"I got into some trouble and I may need you to bail me out."

"No. You want out, call Dad!"

"I can't! He'll kill me."

"Too bad, I told you to stop fucking with those drugs. Bye Kieran."

If it had been my brother's first offense, I may have felt sorry for him—but it wasn't. I didn't have the time or the money to waste on him right now. Once or twice a month, I received calls like this from jail, and since Dad was buddies with the chief, they always allowed him to make bail. It made me quite sick actually. I wished Dad would just teach him a lesson and leave him in there for at least a week, and maybe then he would quit being stupid.

The day had started off exciting and now he'd killed my mood. I put my Nat-Co files into the file cabinet and went to check on Ryan.

He was sitting in the conference room, typing away on his laptop, with his headphones plugged into his ears; I snuck up behind him and yanked them out of his ears. "Oops."

"Hey! What the hell?"

"I ran out of coffee." I said, carefully reaching over his lap with my torso and placing the cup down next to his laptop.

"I-I'll get that for you, right away Ms. Quinn."

"Thanks."

ELEVEN

There was an old abandoned building across the street from my office that had been for sale for quite some time. I'd had my eye on that 'For Sale' sign for as long as I could remember, and had finally decided to put an offer in for it a few weeks before. I already had the contractors at the ready, I just needed to get the building permit.

"Ms. Quinn," Karen said over the intercom.

"Yes?"

"There is a Keith Lee here to see you."

"Send him in please."

A tall, mysterious looking male approached my office door. He wore an all black pinstripe suit, his head was clean-shaven, and his facial stubble was lined up perfectly with his jaw. "Ms. Quinn, I presume?"

The way he pronounced my name sent chills down spine. The deep rasp that escaped his mouth almost paralyzed me in my chair. "Yes, that's me."

He extended his hand out for a handshake, and then sat down in front of my desk. Something about him captivated me and I couldn't look away. His green eyes demanded my full attention. "So, Sheila, you do know that I am the sole person standing between you and that property across the street, right?"

"No. I honestly have no idea who you are or what the fuck you are doing here."

"Oh, I like you already. I'll tell you what, let's skip the small talk. What are you willing to do to get that building?"

"I'm willing to pay for it, like any normal person would!" I said, raising my voice.

"Aw, that's too bad. I liked you, but Ashley Vaughn made a better offer."

Ashley fucking Vaughn, a name I had hoped I wouldn't have to hear again in this life time. She was the niece of my business associate Roger Vaughn and also my ex best friend. We had interned at my dad's company all throughout high school and college together. I busted my ass and worked hard, while she tried to sleep her way to the top. Roger always covered for her, but my father never cut me any slack just because we were related; he wanted me to have morals.

Ashley was such a bitch and if she didn't get her way, she'd cry and whine about it until she finally got what she wanted. She must have heard from her uncle that I was interested in buying that property and decided to sex it into her own greedy grasp. Ever since she found out she wasn't getting a position in this company, she'd been out to get me. Anything that was important to me, that I needed or wanted, she tried to take. *I'll be damned if I let her take this away from me.*

"What do you have in mind, Keith?"

"Well, you are a pretty girl, I'm sure we can work something out," he said with his eyes fixated on my cleavage.

I slowly stood to my feet and seductively walked over to him, placing my hands on his shoulders. I bent down to his ear. "I'll tell you what, you can take me out on a date tonight, and we'll discuss this further. Meet me here at eight p.m. tonight." I kissed him on the cheek, knowing that would help seal the deal.

"I'll be here."

"Good. Now get out of my office."

I stayed in the office all day until it was almost time for my date with Keith. I always left a change of clothes in the coat closet for these last minute outings. We had a private shower on the ground floor by the gym that was usually pretty empty around this time so I figured I wouldn't be disturbed, but I locked the door anyway.

Eight o'clock arrived fast and I made my way to the lobby to wait for him. I would do almost anything to get that building, because it meant a lot to me.

Three years before it had been a huge event planning business. If you wanted a wedding, engagement, birthday, or corporate party, this was the place to go. Liam and I had planned to have our wedding and reception there, but shortly after I called off the engagement, the second floor caught on fire. The previous owners decided to skip town and never fixed it. My crew had already assessed the damage and decided to knock it down and rebuild it. But, in order to do that, I apparently had to go through Keith.

Thirty minutes later, Keith finally made his grand entrance. "Sorry I'm late. I got tied up at the office."

"I'm sure you did, now where are we going?"

"Do you like seafood?"

"Yes."

"Good, we'll go down to Bob's Crab Shack on the waterfront." He grabbed my hand and walked me outside to his double-parked, all black Mercedes.

The view of the waterfront was beautiful. Bright white lights reflected off of it, illuminating the dark waters. We pulled in front of the ranch style building with a huge ugly crab on the front. The exterior looked old, dingy, and weather beaten. Keith opened the door for me and we were immediately greeted by the young hostess. She quickly informed us that there would be a slight delay in seating us because they were still cleaning out a few booths. It made me feel a little bit better about being here, knowing they thoroughly cleaned up after their guests.

I took a moment to look around and admire the scenery. The interior was completely lined with wood. Walls, floors, tables, even the built in bar was made of wood, but it did look up to date.

There were fishing poles, buoys, and all sorts of other sea themed décor hanging from the ceiling. Pictures of beer surrounded the wooden paneling above the bar and the strong smell of fish wafted through the air, causing my stomach to grumble. I hadn't eaten much all day besides a banana and several cups of coffee.

The hostess, a brunette with pig tails, approached us with two menus in hand and escorted us to a booth by the window. "Kay will be with you shortly, enjoy."

The place was very packed for a Wednesday evening. Waitresses in white shirts and black slacks branded with the crab logo were running everywhere trying to keep up. Finally, a tall blonde with pigtails greeted us, "I'm Kay and I'll be taking care of you tonight."

After briefly scoping the menu, I decided to order the shrimp and chips for my entrée and the boiled crab legs for an appetizer. "Wow, where are you going to put all of that," Keith said sarcastically.

"That small amount of food was me being generous. If you prefer, I could order the entire left side of the menu."

"No, no! That's quite all right. I'll have the fried haddock sandwich with fries and the same appetizer as her," he said.

"Anything to drink?" she asked.

"I'll have a Patrón margarita." Keith gazed at me with his deep green eyes and then I ordered for him as well.

"Sheila, why do you want that burned, rundown building anyway? You could have any other property in this entire state, so what makes that one so special?"

"Well, if you want the truth, I was going to have my wedding reception there once upon a time." I looked down at the ground, hoping I'd really sell that to him. I was in fact telling the truth, but I didn't want him to know how much it *really* meant to me.

"I see, well Ashley, has no sentimental attachments to it, but her offer was still a bit better than yours."

"Well after my margaritas kick in, I'm sure we can continue this party elsewhere."

After a nice meal and several bottomless margaritas, I had a nice buzz. I wasn't as intoxicated as I appeared to be, but I had to let Keith believe he was in control. We left the restaurant after he paid for everything and pulled up in front of a cheap one-story motel right off the highway. He parked directly in front of a room and walked around the car to open the door for me. He slid the keycard out of his pocket, which further convinced me that this had been his plan all along.

"Now Sheila, I need to know, are you okay with this?"

"Yes."

"Do you prefer the kinky stuff or a more mild approach at this?"

"As kinky as you'd like," I slurred. He walked over to the closet, pulled out a huge brown paper bag, and sat it on the floor beside him. He then went into the bathroom and I ran over to examine the bag's contents. There was a mask, a rope, a whip, a paddle, handcuffs, and a wax candle. I honestly hadn't pegged him as that level of freaky, but I knew I could handle it.

I quickly ran back over to the neatly made bed, which was covered with a maroon comforter. The room was pretty small with green carpeting and out dated floral wallpaper. Keith returned to the room in a pair of gray boxer briefs. He wasn't overly muscular, but was in decent shape. Dark hair covered his chest and stomach along with his legs.

He walked over to me and placed his hands on either side of my face, slowly tilting my head up toward him. Once he inhaled the scent of my hair, I knew I had to think fast.

He yanked my locks free from their rubber clasp and fluffed the waves down my back. "You should wear your hair out more."

"So I've heard."

He unzipped my dress and brought me to my feet, allowing the material to fall to the floor. He sucked on my neck roughly, then went over to the closet and grabbed the paper bag full of toys. "Wait, you should let me do the honors," I said.

"What would you like me to do?" he asked with a sarcastic yet playful tone.

"Remove your underwear and lie down on your back." He slid his boxers to the floor, releasing his thick but average length member. I removed my undergarments and retrieved the mask, rope, and handcuffs from the bag.

I walked around the side of the bed and slid the mask over his eyes. He tried to grab my tit before I completely covered them and I smacked his hand away. "Don't."

The bed had an old wooden headboard with metal rails underneath. I threaded the rope through them and double tied it to each side of the bed before attaching the handcuffs to his hands. Fully attaching the rope to the handcuffs, I pulled as tight as I could, to properly secure his hands to the board above his head. "Tight enough?" I asked.

"It's perfect."

"Good."

There were a few more pieces of rope left and I used them to clasp around his ankles and attach them to the front rail. "Before we start, do you have the document with you?"

"Yes, and I already signed it."

"That's a good boy, where is it?"

"In my front pocket, but I don't get what that has to do with us right now."

"Oh, nothing," I said, climbing on top of him and giving him a deep, passion filled kiss.

"I love a girl that takes charge of her man."

"Now, I want you to relax. I'm going to take real good care of you." I kissed him from his lips down his chest, and then climbed off his body, positioning myself right next to him.

I grabbed hold of his cock and slowly started massaging it, quickly making it hard as a rock. Up and down, faster than slower, I played with it. I jerked his erection until it released all over my hand. "I'll be right back."

I went into the bathroom and saw his jacket behind the door. I grabbed it and the document was nowhere to be found. After quickly washing my hands, I spotted his pants on the floor. I picked them up and there it was, in his right pocket—*signed*. I also grabbed a souvenir for good measure.

I exited the room and placed the paper on the floor next to my clothes. Then I walked over to him and whispered in his ear, "The safe word is, corporate."

"Ooh, I like safe words. Do your worst!"

"Oh, I will." I said, quickly redressing myself. I tucked the document into my bra along with his wallet for safe keeping.

"Bye, Keith."

"Wait, where are you going?"

"I'm leaving, but don't worry, I'll be back—eventually."

I walked down to the front office and asked the owner if I could use his fax machine and copier. I needed to make sure I had my own personal copy of this signed document, and I copied his information just for the hell of it. I knew Ryan would be in the office first thing in the morning and that he'd put it aside for me without question.

After everything was sent, I went back to the room to check on Keith. I was sure he was freaking out by then.

Before I let myself back in I heard him cursing and trying to free himself from the restraints. "Calm down princess, I'm back. What kind of devious bitch do you think I am?"

"I don't know. I wasn't sure if you were coming back, you scared me for a minute."

"I know, it was pretty fun actually, to fuck with you like that."

I went into the bathroom and placed his empty wallet back into his pants.

"Well Keith, it was fun getting to know you, but I really do have to get going now."

"Wait? What? Sheila, where are you going? You can kiss that fucking building goodbye if you walk out of that door!" he roared at me.

"Kiss my ass, Keith. I already have everything I want. I'll make sure you lie there long and *hard* until housekeeping finds you in the morning."

"You bitch!" he yelled, ferociously trying to free himself from his restraints.

"That's Mrs. Bitch to you. And Keith, I better never see your fucking face again, you twisted pig."

TWELVE

"So, Sheila, I placed those documents in your office, right on top of your desk."

"Thank you, Ryan."

"I checked the time stamp and it was well after midnight when you faxed them. Where were you?"

"I was out, handling some personal business."

"I see," he said with a discouraged tone.

"I do have some good news though."

"What?"

"I got the permit! They'll start reconstruction tomorrow."

"Oh, well that calls for a celebration!"

"Ryan, I don't know it's—"

"Quit being such a baby! It'll be fun. Besides, everyone knew how important it was that you got that building. Why? I don't know, but I'm sure you worked really hard and you need to loosen up a bit."

"Fine. Now get out of my office, I have paperwork to sign."

"Okay. Oh and Sheila, you have a little something there on your neck."

I hurried into my office, shut the door, and grabbed my compact mirror out of my purse. There it was: a fucking *hickey*. I quickly applied my powdered foundation to cover it up; I didn't need anyone else pointing it out.

Every time I went out with Ryan, I felt alive. I felt safe, as if no one could do me any harm. No matter where we went together, I felt like it was just us in the room. That night we decided to try a local club and everything about it was just awful.

The bar was in need of a serious update. It had wooden columns in the middle of the floor, bricks were missing from the walls, and the front of the actual bar had cracks and duct tape sealing up the improvements. It also reeked of urine and the stench of death.

"Let's get out of here!" Ryan yelled in my ear.

"Where to?"

"My place."

We arrived in front of his apartment and for some odd reason, I didn't think it was a good idea. Usually when I had a feeling like this, I didn't ignore it.

"Hey Ryan, I think I'm gonna go. I'll see you in the office tomorrow."

"Are you sure? I mean, we just got here."

"Yes, see you tomorrow." He looked discouraged, but I just wasn't feeling it.

On my way back to my condo, I decided to call Liam. I felt like he should know that I'd bought that property.

"Hello?"

"Hey, Liam."

"Sheila? Is everything all right?"

"Yeah, I just wanted to tell you that I am now the owner of the old Bernstein property."

"The place we were supposed to have our wedding?"

"Yes," I said sternly, trying to hold back any emotion.

"Wow, I don't know what to say. I didn't think you still cared."

"I don't, but I didn't want to see the property go to waste."

"Quinny, you can cut the tough guy act with me. Come over and see me. I don't think you should be alone tonight."

Ever since I left him, I'd had this insatiable craving. This need—this dark desire—for sex. I slept with strangers for a cheap thrill, hoping they could satisfy me the way he did, but none of them could make my body feel like Liam could. I tried to bury my feelings for him, deep down inside of my soul, but they kept coming back to the surface.

As I drove to his condo, my stomach turned, and my palms were starting to sweat as I tightly clutched the steering wheel.

Liam was sitting on the front steps when I arrived. He was wearing a pair of jeans and was shirtless. He came down the stairs and walked around the front of my car, opening the driver side door for me. He didn't say one word to me. He just unhooked my seat belt, grabbed my hand, and led me inside. "Liam, I—"

He slammed the door shut behind us and charged at me, ramming my back against the wall. He lifted my body into the air, still pinning me against the wall, and ripped my panties free from underneath my dress. Quickly dropping his pants, he shoved himself up into me, and before I could even attempt to fight him off, my body gave in. Our eyes met for a brief moment and that's when I realized: he was *still* in love with me.

Pressing his head against my face, he plowed himself deeper inside my walls, making my body quiver from the intense pleasure.

This is what I needed, what I missed.

THIRTEEN

"Ms Quinn, you look—*different*. Did you have a good time last night?" Rose asked.

"I guess you could say that. The whole day was great, to be honest with you."

"Good, well you have a present on your desk."

I was already certain that it was from Liam, most likely some type of celebratory flowers, but I was in shock when I finally stepped into my office.

A large fruit bouquet was sitting in the middle of my desk, with flowers and a card. I walked over to pick up the card, and inside it said *Congratulations on the permit, you rock Ms. Quinn!*

It was from Ryan, not Liam. I was a little shocked that Ryan would do this, seeing as I'd blatantly blown him off the night before. But, it was a very sweet gesture.

"Knock, knock. I see you got my gift! You don't look too impressed though. Did I go over the top? Do you not like pineapple?" Ryan asked.

"No, no! It's fine, I just—"

"Just, what? You thought it was from someone else didn't you?"

"Yes, I did."

"Oh, well, here's your coffee."

"Thank you Li—I mean Ryan. It was very sweet of you." As he turned around to leave my office, he sported the look of sheer embarrassment and sadness. A part of me felt bad, but there was nothing I could do. I thought what I thought and I wasn't changing my mind for anyone.

I sat down at my desk, staring at the fruit bouquet, and Karen interrupted me over the intercom. "Ms. Quinn, you have a special delivery."

"Oh god, what now?"

Several large flower arrangements came through my door. A note was stuck to the last one:

FOR THE WOMAN THAT STILL CARES, FROM THE MAN
THAT NEVER STOPPED.

I decided to take Ryan out that night, as a thank you for all of his help. He'd worked harder for me than any other intern I'd ever encountered.

"Ms. Quinn, you didn't have to do this. I just really admire your work, and enjoy being able to work for you."

"I know, Ryan, but I value you as a trusted employee and have a surprise for you tonight."

I drove us to a fancy five star Italian restaurant. It was one of my favorite places to go with my father. Their cheesy breadsticks were to die for, and don't get me started on their house wine selection.

I was a VIP member there and already had reservations in place for us. I came in and gave the hostess my card and she immediately got us a booth in the back of the restaurant.

I opened my purse and handed Ryan a card. "Open it."

He tore the envelope open like a kid on Christmas, and as soon as he read what was inside his facial expression changed. "Ms. Quinn, are you serious?"

"I'm serious, Ryan. You are Quinn National's newest employee, unless you have other plans."

"No, this just means so much; I've only been with your company for a few months."

"Yes, and in those short months, you've made our computers run faster, kept everything neatly filed, and sent me everything in virtual file folders. So this decision was a no-brainer. And it doesn't hurt that you enjoy the night life like I do and make a mean cup of coffee."

"Thank you, so much!"

"You're welcome, and Ryan?"

"Yes?"

"Shots on me!"

Several hours later, Ryan and I were both highly intoxicated. I hailed us a cab, left my car in the parking lot, and arranged a tow to bring it back to my place.

"Shee, can I stay over your house tonight? I don't want to go home," he said with a slur.

"Sure." I handed the cab driver a piece of paper with my address on it and he nodded at me in the rear view mirror.

Ryan and I both nodded off during the ride, and the cab driver had to come around and open the door for us, gently tapping me on the shoulder. "We're here ma'am."

"Thank you so much. Let's go Ryan," I said, handing the driver a fifty-dollar tip while attempting to push Ryan out of the cab.

We walked up the stars to my condo and once I opened the door, Ryan plopped down on the black leather couch. "Are you okay?" I asked.

"Yes, I just need some water, but I should be serving you."

"It's fine Ryan, we're not at work anymore."

I went into the fridge and pulled out two bottles of water, quickly returning to the living room and handing him one.

He opened the bottle, took a sip, and placed it on the glass coffee table. Turning to me, he pushed me back on the couch. "Ryan, what are you doing?"

"I thought this was what you wanted."

"If I wanted it, I would have had it already. I think you should lie down and get some rest." Embarrassed, he slid his shoes off under the coffee table and lay back on the couch. I went into the hall closet to get him a blanket and before I made it back into the room, he was knocked out cold.

In due time my friend, in due time.

FOURTEEN

Having shut him down the night before, I was a little skeptical about going back into the living room in the morning. Although nothing had happened between us, that awkward sexual tension would still be there. I grabbed my robe from my bedside and slid it over my shoulders, tying it around my waist.

I went into the hallway, peering around the wall. He wasn't there. "Ryan?" I said as I walked into the living room. He was gone and there was a note on the coffee table.

SHEILA, I HAD TO RUN, I'LL SEE YOU AT WORK LATER.

–RYAN

I crumpled the note up and went back into my room to get ready for work.

I pulled into the garage and greeted the attending officer, "Hey, Bill." I took the elevator upstairs and found that everyone seemed to be in a great mood.

"Hey, Sheila!" Ryan said, handing me a hot mug of coffee. "The building contractor faxed over the last of the paperwork and needs you to call him as soon as it's completed."

"Thanks," I said, wondering why he had handed me a mug of coffee rather than leaving it on my desk. I went into my office and hung my jacket on the rack. While placing my briefcase and the mug on the table, I noticed another note on my desk.

SORRY ABOUT LAST NIGHT, SOMETIMES I GET A LITTLE

CRAZY WHEN I DRINK TOO MUCH—FORGIVE ME. –RYAN

Tossing it into the shredder, I opened the folder full of contracts and paperwork and signed my life away.

I called Jacob, the contractor, and told him I'd meet with him in an hour to discuss things further.

"Jacob, everything is coming along nicely. How much longer do you think this project will take to complete?"

"About six more months at the latest. This is by far one of the easiest projects I've ever worked on."

"Thanks, I'll see you then. Oh and I expect you to be at the big reveal and launch party."

"Thank you for the invite, I will most certainly be there."

On my way back to my condo, my phone rang. "Hello?"

"Sheila, you've got to get to the hospital now, it's Dad!" I didn't need any other explanation; I knew something bad had to have happened for my older sister Shannon to call me. There was only one hospital he trusted with his life: The Deacon.

"Excuse me, what room is Mr. Quinn in?" I asked the receptionist in a panic.

"He's currently in the ICU; he just came out of emergency surgery."

"Emergency surgery for what?" I asked, puzzled.

"I'm not sure, but he's on the tenth floor. You can take the L1 elevator around the corner."

I quickly ran to the elevator and banged on the up arrow until the elevator finally got back to my floor. One person was inside and I nearly knocked him over trying to rush in.

I felt like time slowed down as the elevator took its sweet time to get to my floor. My father meant everything to me, and I couldn't risk losing him—not right now, not *ever.*

My sister was standing in the hallway waiting for me and filled me in before we walked into the room. She held my hand and calmly said, "Dad had a heart attack. The doctors found a small blockage in one of his main arteries, but they were able to surgically repair it. He's resting now, so please don't disturb him."

"Shut up, Shannon." I walked into the room and almost cried at the sight. Dad was on his back in bed, with tubes up his nose and wires hanging from his arms. His skin was starting to regain its caramel color and his salt and pepper hair and mustache were still well groomed.

I walked over to him and gently lifted his hand, placing a kiss on top of his knuckles. I knew he was going to be okay, but I wanted to say a short D'ua, a Muslim prayer, as I moved my hand to his heart. I recited it several times in Arabic, then once in English. "Dear Lord, please remove this pain and cure it. You are the only one who can truly remove this illness and I leave it in your hands."

My father was the only person I would say this for. When we were younger, Mom made us perform a Salat, which was a daily prayer that needed to be completed five times a day. Once we came to the States, we no longer practiced it as religiously as we had before. We also used to pray in groups every Friday, but that was another ritual we lost moving to a new place.

After my prayer, I told Shannon to keep in touch with me and also left my number with the nurse. If there were any changes, or if things went wrong, I wanted to be the first to know.

Seeing Dad like that did upset me quite a bit and I had to let off some steam. I picked up my phone and made a call.

"Ryan, are you free tonight?"

"For you, I'm always free."

I picked Ryan up and brought him to a nearby hotel. The things I wanted to do to him needed to be done outside of our homes. We stopped in the bar and took a few shots, and brought a huge bottle of vodka and cola upstairs with us. I handed him the keycard to slide, and entered the room behind him.

"Sheila, may I ask what's wrong? You don't seem like yourself tonight."

"Does it matter? Does life *really* matter?" I said in a drunken rage.

"Yes it does, it always does. Did something bad happen?"

I couldn't fight it anymore. The tears fell free from my eyes and onto the floor beneath me. He wrapped his arms around me and kissed the top of my head. "It's okay Sheila. You don't have to tell me right now. I'll go make us some more drinks."

I plopped down on the bed and the room started to spin. Ryan came over with a cup full of vodka and cola and I chugged the whole thing back. I needed to numb this pain as soon as possible.

FIFTEEN

My dad was released from the hospital after a two-week stay in the intensive care unit. A home health aide was ordered to be at his beck and call until he was back to a hundred percent. I was so thankful that the doctors were able to diagnose him right away, because if anything had happened to him in their care, I would have completely lost it.

Ryan and I swore to never bring up that pathetic night in the hotel again. I really had planned on sexing him into oblivion, not crying in his fucking lap all night. I was really starting to trust him a lot. We had a ton of fun outside of work, but at work, we kept everything strictly professional.

I finally gave Ryan his own office directly across from mine so that I could keep an eye on him at all times. Occasionally I caught myself staring at him as he typed away on his keyboard. With his new position, he also scanned all documents and uploaded them to the new computers we'd bought. He kept teasing me about the 'outdated' system, so I'd finally done something about it—with his help of course.

One night we were both so caught up in our work that I didn't even realize it was after ten p.m. I had emptied every single file I had in my cabinet and brought it over to him to upload to the computer, except for one.

As I walked across the hall, I noticed he had removed his suit jacket and unbuttoned a few clasps on his shirt, revealing his smooth, defined chest underneath. I felt a small pulse under my skirt and knew I couldn't fight these urges any longer.

I tapped on the door, "Hey, Ryan?"

"Yeah?" he said looking up at me with his piercing blue eyes.

"I have one more folder for you." I walked over to his desk slowly and placed the file on top of it. I sat down next to the folder and crossed my legs.

"Ms—uh—" he said nervously. "Is there anything else I can do for you?"

"In fact, there is." I slid off the desk to my feet and pushed him back in the chair, running my fingers down his shirt.

I pressed my chest against his and slid down his body, spreading his legs as I kneeled before him. It didn't take much for him to become aroused, and his bulge was quite noticeable underneath his slacks.

I ran my hand over it, slowly caressing it through the fabric. I ran my lips across it, feeling it throb under his pants.

Reaching for his buckle, I unfastened it and unzipped his pants, freeing his cock from his boxers. "Sheila…" Before he could continue, I slid my mouth over the head of it. As I swirled my tongue around the tip, his body started to tense up.

I relaxed my throat to try to accommodate his girth but it wouldn't fit, so I used my hand to assist me. Up and down my hand slid, in sync with my lips, until I felt his body tense. I removed my lips and finished him off with my hand.

I got up off my knees and went out the office door, heading to the bathroom down the hall to wash my hands. Before I made it inside, Ryan ran up behind me, pushed me in and locked the door behind us. He shoved my back up against the door and his lips crashed into mine. I opened my mouth, allowing his tongue to fully slide in.

He raised my arms above my head and pinned them against the door, locking them in place with one hand as he used his free hand to reach underneath my skirt and slide my panties down to the floor. Then he released my hands just long enough to drop his pants and slide on a condom.

Lifting me into the air, he slowly inched his cock inside of me, carefully letting my walls stretch to receive him—all of him. His tongue traced the side of my neck as he began to pick up speed.

Faster and faster he thrust, smacking my back against the door. I wrapped my legs around him tightly, enjoying every single stroke.

My body heated and my legs started to quake. I could feel myself getting closer. His breathing sped up and his strokes slowed down. I felt him getting closer too.

I let out a loud moan, and he slammed me into the door one last time, causing us both to climax together. He paused briefly before he released me from the wall and kissed me again before tossing the rubber in the trash and fastening his pants.

As he washed his hands, he looked at me in the mirror and said, "Don't worry, no one will ever know about this," and left the bathroom. I walked over to the mirror, fixed my hair, and re adjusted my skirt. I turned around to retrieve my panties, but they were gone.

I ran down the hall back to his office and saw him with them pressed against his nose, inhaling my scent. "Looking for something?" he said.

"Yes, you can hand them over now," I demanded.

"There's nothing stopping you from coming to get them," he retorted.

"Keep them. That way when you go home and beat off later, you'll have a souvenir."

As I lay in my bed I couldn't stop thinking about Ryan and what we'd done in the bathroom. All the sexual tension that had built up between us had been released, and I craved more.

My phone vibrated on the night stand and I saw two messages. One was my dad letting me know he was okay and not to worry. The other was from Ryan. It was a photo of my black lace thong.

I laughed at the thought of Ryan actually keeping my underwear. I'd figured he'd just toss them, unless sniffing used thongs was his past time.

SIXTEEN

On my way into work I couldn't stop thinking about what Ryan and I had done.

My body still tingled and craved him. Liam had been the only person my body hungered for like that, until now.

As I walked though the office door a bright idea came to me. I needed to write a press release about my national gas project. It was the only way to generate huge hype and sell it to consumers without shoving it down their throats.

I'd ask Karen to set up an interview with Channel Five News and I'd have Ryan help me with the press release. I really believed in our natural gas project division and believed it could eventually benefit everyone.

"Hey Ryan, are you any good with press releases?"

"I've never dealt with one before, but I don't think it would be very hard to figure out."

"Good, I'll write up a rough draft while you do some research."

Ryan and I stayed in the office all night long trying to perfect the press release. I really felt it was going to make a huge impact on consumers.

I was going to rebrand this company and this was step one.

"I'm starving, Sheila. Would you like me to order some Chinese food or something?"

"Sure, don't forget the lomein and crab rangoon," I said, faking a smile.

I wasn't a huge fan of Chinese food this late at night and I knew I was going to pay for it in the morning.

After our quick greasy meal, we finally perfected the letter. It was after two a.m. when we finished.

"Thanks for your help, Ryan."

"It wasn't a problem, Sheila."

I left the conference room to lock my things up in my office. Once I was finished I sat down and watched Ryan from across the hall.

His sleeves were rolled up to his elbows and his hair was a mess from constantly running his fingers through it all night in frustration.

The more I admired him from afar, the more I wanted him, the more my body wanted him.

"Hey Ryan, could you come here for a moment?"

"Sure, be there in a sec." I hiked my skirt up and sat on top of my desk, waiting.

"Yes Sheila?" he said, slowly entering the room.

"Shut the door behind you," I commanded.

He shut the door and then walked over to me. I grabbed a hold of his shirt and unbuttoned all of his clasps.

Revealing his slim, toned physique underneath, I ran my fingers up and down his six pack while he stood idle with his hands by his sides.

I slid off of the desk to my feet and kissed the base of his neck. He tilted his head back while I continued my journey further down his body, slowly taunting him, inch-by-inch, until I returned to my feet.

"Ryan, look into my eyes," I said while grasping the back of his neck and pressing my body up against his.

His blue eyes bore into mine and I felt his cock pressing up against his pants. The tension between us was very high. "Kiss me, Ryan."

His lips forcefully crashed upon mine as he pushed me back on top of my desk.

He spread my legs apart and slid his hand in between them, immediately feeling my wetness. "No panties, tonight?" he asked.

"I figured I wouldn't be needing them."

He laughed then unbuttoned my shirt, displaying my lace push up bra and noticeable cleavage.

Nuzzling his face in between them, he reached behind me and unhooked it, letting my heavy breasts fall free. "God, you're beautiful," he whispered.

His lips made contact with my nipples, slowly pulling each one into his mouth. His lips traveled further down my skin, setting my body on fire.

Once his lips made contact with my opening, I knew I was putty in his hands. Each swirl of his tongue caused my body to seize with pleasure. Chills went up my spine as I grasped hold of his hair. He locked his lips on my clit and as much as I tried to fight it, he made my body quiver.

He climbed back on top of me and kissed me, sharing the flavor of my pussy with me. Breaking our kiss momentarily, he ripped open a condom and slid it on his throbbing cock.

Grabbing hold of the back of my neck, slowly he entered me, staring deeply into my eyes with each stroke, torturing my body.

His eyes were full of hope and I knew I had him right where I wanted him.

"She—" he whispered.

"Ryan, don't."

"I—" His body slightly trembled and he pulled out of me, trying to hold back the sensation to come. He calmly stoked his cock and re entered me, thrusting harder than he ever had before.

My eyes started to roll into the back of my head as I lost total control of my body.

His hand gripped my neck once more and his stare was intense. He was focused, focused on making me come, and I did, just before he did.

I sat up on the desk staring at him. His abs twitched as he slid his pants back up. He ran his hand across his mouth, wiping away my left over residue, and smiled.

"I'll see you tomorrow, Ryan."

SEVENTEEN

Ryan was a great worker and a damn good fuck, but the look in his eyes when we were together showed me he was looking for something I had no interest in: *a commitment.*

Liam was a big part of the reason why I shut myself down. I'd given up so much for him that I'd lost myself. I'd lost sight of what *I* wanted.

I became more like my dad. I wanted to love my work, build an empire, and then eventually settle down and share my life with someone, but it wasn't the time for that.

Now it was all about my needs, not my wants.

I decided to go into work late the next day. After the late night with Ryan, I figured I'd earned it. Our letter was perfect and had been sent out the night before, after our little rendezvous.

As I rolled over in bed, my phone vibrated. I looked at the screen and saw a text from Liam.

> *Liam: Are you working today?*

> *Me: Not at the moment, but I will be, why?*

> *Liam: Good, open the door.*

I had no idea what he wanted and it was even more of a shock that he was in front of my place. I grabbed my robe and headed to the front door.

I looked through my peep hole and he was standing right in front of the door with something behind his back. I couldn't see what it was, but I figured it was flowers.

As I unlocked the top latch my heart started beating rapidly. I was nervous, but why? I had no reason to be nervous. Besides, he was in my space, not a foreign place.

"Good morning, Sheila," he said as he handed me a styrofoam coffee cup. "I'll be right back."

He ran back down the stairs and to his car. He grabbed a couple styrofoam trays and a bouquet of flowers, then returned to my door.

"What's all this?"

"Breakfast. I plan on having you for lunch."

We sat down at the bar in the kitchen and I opened my tray. It was full of diced hash browns, turkey sausage, and egg whites.

"Thank you, Liam. You didn't have to do this."

"Of course I did. You deserve so much more than just breakfast from me."

I could feel my cheeks start to heat as I stuck my fork into my potatoes.

After breakfast, I invited him over to the couch to watch a movie, but we never got the chance to watch anything. As soon as we sat on the couch he shoved me back, loosened the tie on my robe, and fucked me—*raw.*

Thank god I was still on birth control, because the last thing I needed right now was a baby. A baby brought into this stressful ass world would not be good, especially if it was Liam's.

After having breakfast and experiencing Liam for lunch, I finally strolled into the office around noon. Ryan was looking at me suspiciously, like he knew I'd been with someone else. He never said anything about it, but the look on his face told me exactly what he was thinking.

"Hey Ryan, did you hear anything back from the press regarding our release?"

"Not yet. I'm sure they were so stunned at its perfection that they need some more time to process it all."

"I sure hope so. Could you order lunch for us?"

"Sure, what would you like?"

"A grilled chicken Caesar salad, with light dressing on the side."

I sat down at my desk and saw a huge manila folder on it. Inside were more permits and health and safety information in regards to natural gas. I started to regret coming in so late; if I had come in first thing in the morning all that paperwork would be finished already.

As I tackled the stacks of papers, Ryan came in with lunch. "That was fast."

"Let's just say I kind of ordered it ahead of time. I figured you'd order a salad anyway," he laughed.

"Well, you must know me very well, then."

"Indeed I do, Ms. Quinn. I know more about you than you care to realize."

The creepy smile that formed on his face at that moment would normally freak any girl out, but not me. The only thing that could scare me would be my father passing away, and I knew that wasn't happening any time soon.

I devoured my salad and dove right back in to my paperwork. I was determined to have it all signed, sent, and filed before the normal work day was over.

73

Several hours later, I finally finished my paperwork just before the clock struck six o'clock.

I placed the stack of papers back in the folder for Ryan to scan and file for me. As I walked across the hall, he was nowhere to be found. I placed the folder down on his desk and went back to my office. Usually he was always there, and normally I wouldn't care, but I was a little curious since the office was getting ready to close for the weekend.

I grabbed my phone out of my purse and texted him.

Me: Where are you?

No answer. All of his things were still in the office, so I assumed he must have run out for a minute. I wasn't going to dwell on it, but I was going to leave at seven with or without him.

Thirty minutes passed and there was still no sign of Ryan. I decided to take a walk and look for him. I brought my cell phone just in case he messaged me during my search.

I took the elevator to the ground floor and walked by the gym. *Bingo!*

Ryan was inside the gym with his headphones in, pumping away on the arm cruncher machine. He had a black sleeveless undershirt on and the sweat from his continuous reps was pouring down his face. He looked hot, I had to admit. I hadn't pegged him for a person to hit the gym like this, so it was a little surprising to say the least.

As I stalked from afar, my cell phone rang and Liam's number was on my screen.

"Yes?"

"What are you up to right now?"

"Nothing much, why?" I asked.

"I wanted to take you out for dinner tonight. Do you have plans?"

I looked over at Ryan and he stopped working out. Our eyes connected through the glass and he started smiling. "I do have plans tonight. We can go out another time, bye."

Ryan waved for me to come inside the gym with him. I opened the door and the smell of sweat filled the air. "Like what you saw?"

"Maybe. I had no idea you even knew what a gym was," I joked.

"Guess we both learn something new about each other every day, huh?"

"I guess so. Would you like to go for a run with me tomorrow morning?" I asked.

"Sure. What time?"

"Six o'clock sharp, not a minute later. Meet me at the reservoir!"

"Six in the morning?" he questioned.

"Yes."

"I'll be there. Don't you worry."

EIGHTEEN

I set my alarm for four a.m. to prepare for my run with Ryan. I always completely stretched my body out before a run and made sure I ate or drank a high energy, low fat snack to keep me going.

My goal was to run five miles with him; I decided to keep it light for his first run with me. I could easily run ten miles in my sleep, but wanted to see if he could keep up with me.

Running was an escape for me. I put on my spanks and tank top, plugged in my headphones, and tucked my blade in my bra, just because I trusted no one.

When my feet hit that pavement, I felt like it was me against the world. Some of my best business ideas came to me while I was out for a run. All my stress left my body through my soles and was left behind me, allowing me to open my mind and think freely.

I power walked to the reservoir and got there fairly early. Not many people were out at that time of morning, but there was a strange guy in a gray hooded sweat shirt sitting on the bench in front of the water.

I had left my phone at home and hoped Ryan got my text, but I hadn't bothered checking before I left.

I walked over to a tree to help me balance as I did one final stretch of my calves to make sure I was nice and loose. I couldn't help but feel like I was being watched and as I turned around, the hooded stranger was behind me.

I stepped back and started reaching for my blade. He slid his hood back to reveal himself. "Ryan? I almost stabbed you!"

"Well good morning to you, too," he laughed.

"No one is usually here at this time, especially not hanging out on a bench with a hood over their head like some creep."

"Hey, did we come here to run or to dwell on my creepiness?"

"Both, actually," I laughed.

"How many miles are we running today?" he questioned.

"I figured we'd start with five."

He shook his head in disgust at me. "Seriously, Sheila? I can tell you run ten miles easy. Your body is in phenomenal shape."

"You're right; I wanted to take it easy on you."

"Sheila please, I used to run cross country. I'll have no problem keeping up with you. Besides, when did you start getting soft?"

"Soft? Okay Mr. Cross Country, hope you enjoy all uphill!"

An hour and a half later we completed our tenth mile. I was a little sweaty but otherwise fully energized. Ryan looked the same, *surprisingly*.

"I've never met a girl that barely broke a sweat after running ten straight miles."

"Good, and you'll probably never meet another. I'm starving, are you?"

"Yes."

"I could really use a light meal."

"Let's go to my place, Sheila. I'll cook something for us."

"One meal, then I'm leaving, Ryan."

"Deal."

The last time we were at his place, I hadn't really gotten a chance to take in my surroundings. This time I wanted to make sure to scope out the place. As soon as we walked through the front door, the brown leather couch was to the right in a small living space. A mini wooden coffee table was in front of it and a few feet across the room a TV was mounted on the wall. The kitchen was about an arm's length away from the TV. It was clean with updated black appliances and two small counters. There was an archway across from the front door that led down a narrow hallway to his bedroom and the bathroom. The place was way too minuscule for me, but if I were a twenty-two -year -old college kid, it would be like home. "I'll be right back, Ryan."

I placed my purse down on the couch and took a stroll down the tight hallway. My first stop was the bathroom. I turned the light on and everything felt too condensed in the cramped space. There was a stand up shower with no bathtub, a toilet, and a wooden rack he'd put over the toilet as a make shift storage place. Next I went into his bedroom.

I stood in his bedroom, trying to see if I recognized anything in here from the last time, but I didn't. *How fucked up was I?*

I started to poke around his dresser when a small black book titled "Work" caught my eye. Before I could open it, Ryan called me back into the kitchen. As much as I wanted to look through the book, I didn't want to pry right now and get busted.

After my brief tour, I went back into the kitchen to play nice. "Something smells amazing in here."

"I wasn't sure what you ate post workout, but I figured grilled chicken breast, brown rice, and broccoli would be a safe bet."

"It's fine, it looks delicious. You were able to make all of this that fast?"

"No, the chicken was the only thing I cooked right now. Everything else was made before I met with you at the reservoir." He served us both and handed me a bottle of water. "Enjoy."

I cut into the first chicken breast and it was tender and juicy. I placed the first bite in my mouth and couldn't stop. Bite after bite disappeared and tasted better than the one before it as I cleared my plate.

"Thank you, that was really good. But, I should be going now."

"Okay, would you like a ride home?"

"No, I need to walk this delicious meal off. You did give me two pieces of chicken after all." He walked over to me and wrapped his arms around me before I left. I pulled away before I did something I'd regret.

NINETEEN

Tragedy struck Quinn National that day. Our beloved vice president James Tempura suddenly passed away in his sleep overnight. My dad had never been the emotional type, but I could see the hurt in his bloodshot eyes when he came over to tell me the bad news before work. James had been fairly young, and only in his late forties. He'd always taken care of himself, so none of us had seen this coming at all.

Now in addition to Nat-Co, I had the pleasure of hiring a new VP for the company. James had set the bar pretty high and my expectations for a replacement were even higher. Not just any Joe Schmuck was going to get this position. They'd have a lot to prove before I entrusted part of the company to them.

James' funeral was short and sweet. Only his immediate family and a few of his coworkers were present.

"Sheila, don't let your emotions get the best of you. This is sad, but you still have a company to run. Tomorrow you'll need to start searching for a well qualified candidate," said Dad.

"I know, Dad, I'm fine. I just didn't expect this right now. You of all people can understand everything that's on my plate right now. But, all excuses aside, it'll be taken care of."

"Good," he retorted.

"You should get home, Dad. I'll be in touch." He kissed me on the cheek and stepped into his limo.

I found my BMW in a sea of cars and headed to the nearest bar. I texted Ryan to hold down the fort for me until I returned.

I pulled in front of Sam's Bar & Grille, went inside, and found an empty stool in front of the bar. Nothing interesting was on the TV so I looked at my phone and deleted some old emails. The bartender asked me what I'd like and promptly returned with the birthday cake shot I asked for. I chugged the sweet liquid back and returned my gaze to my phone until an unfamiliar voice grabbed my attention.

"What's a beautiful lady like you doing here all alone?"

"Drowning my sorrows with booze, you?"

"The same. My name is John, John Keegan, by the way."

"Sheila."

"Well, Sheila, can I buy you another round?"

"Sure, why the hell not?"

John was gorgeous; he actually looked more like a model than anything else. His short dark hair was tapered on the sides and spiked on the top. Dark stubble perfectly lined his square jaw, his hazel eyes sparkled, and his outfit looked neatly pressed. His white shirt was rolled up to his elbows and his black and gray vest was form fitting, leaving little to the imagination. It was obvious he worked out.

The bartender brought me two shots and handed John a beer.

"So Sheila, what sorrows are you drowning?"

"You first."

"Well. The company I worked for just let me and my entire division go, due to good ole budget cuts."

"Damn that sucks."

"It truly does. I had recently applied for a higher position in the company, so this couldn't have come at a worse time."

"Wow, that's shitty. Well the VP of my company died last week, so there's that."

"Wow, that's equally shitty," he laughed.

"I know, and if I don't fill the position soon, my dad will have my ass."

"Good luck with that."

John and I talked for hours, until my phone exploded with texts and calls from Ryan. "Shit, I have to go."

"You take care of yourself, Sheila. If you ever need a friend, don't hesitate to call me." He pulled a card out of his wallet and handed it to me.

In my mind I wanted to be friends with benefits, but we'd save that for another time. "Thanks, I'll be in touch."

"Sheila, where have you been?" Ryan questioned.

"I was out, calm down."

"Have you been drinking?"

"Yes *Mom*. After the funeral, I went to the bar. Is that a crime?" Ryan became more and more flustered with every prying question.

"Oh Sheila, what am I gonna do with you?"

"I'll be fine. So what's the emergency you blew my phone up for?"

"I've got bad news. There was an accident at one of the drilling sites."

"Are you serious? What kind of 'accident' are we talking about?"

"There was an explosion, and two of the workers received second degree burns."

"How did that happen?"

"I don't have the full report yet, but once I do you will be the first to know."

I stepped into my office and tried to collect myself. I expected a minor hiccup to happen around the office, but I was not prepared to deal with a potential lawsuit. The phone rang as I sat away from my desk, staring out the window. I didn't feel like talking to anyone at the moment, I just wanted the workers who were hurt to recover and either get on with their lives or return to work if they were able to. We've never had a serious accident like this before, at least not to my knowledge, and if the first one happened under my command, word would spread fast and my dad would shit a brick.

"Ryan!" I yelled.

"Yes, Ms. Quinn?"

"Call the site and find out what exactly happened right now. We need to get this handled before word gets out. I need any details you can pry out of them!"

"Right away."

"Shut the door behind you."

I looked through my phone to find the company lawyer's phone number; I wanted to call him and give him a heads up before shit hit the fan.

"Hey Lawrence, it's Sheila. Two workers were hurt during an explosion at one of our sites. I don't have all the information now, but as soon as I do, you'll be the first to know.

TWENTY

"So Terrance, what qualities can you offer us here at Quinn National?"

"Well I have a business degree in marketing, and I brought in over a hundred grand in new revenue working for Clyde & Shaw marketing firm."

"If you were doing so well there, why should I offer you the position here?"

"Because I believe I have a lot to offer. I recently heard you were introducing natural gas here. I believe I can effectively target customers and recruit a large percentage of Massachusetts to convert."

I didn't believe a word Terrance was saying. He hadn't taken his eyes off of my breasts since he walked through the door. I'd done a background check on him the night before and I hadn't found anything significantly unique about him. I'd also called his previous employer and found out he was fired for reporting false revenue accumulated through the company. So I could have told him to fuck off before he sat down at my desk, but I wanted to hear what bullshit he was going to feed me.

"Thank you for your time, I will not be in touch."

The look on his face was priceless. He mumbled the word 'bitch' under his breath on the way out.

"That's Mrs. Bitch to you, asshole!"

Ryan came running into my office with a huge grin on his face. "That bad?"

"I knew his ass was lying before he set foot in my office. Thank god he was my last interview of the day. Tomorrow better bring someone exciting or you'll have to learn marketing."

"So do you have any plans for the night?" Ryan asked.

"I actually do. Shocking, I know."

"Oh, well have a good time, Sheila." Ryan exited my office like a sad puppy. I almost felt bad, but I had a date with John and I needed to get a taste of him before he started his potential new job.

John and I met up at the Illegally Delicious Seafood restaurant. He was standing in front of the glass doors sporting a blue collared shirt and a pair of dark wash jeans. "Wow, I almost didn't recognize you in normal people attire," I joked.

"Same here, although you didn't veer too far off course. Your legs still look exquisite in that leather skirt."

He opened the door for me and as soon as we fought through the crowd, the little buzzer in John's pocket lit up. We went straight to the hostess and she crossed John's name off the waiting list before grabbing two menus.

"So how long have you been waiting here?"

"Don't worry about that beautiful, I just wanted to make sure *you* didn't have to wait too long to be seated."

The hostess seated us in a booth near the window. The seats were soft and made of a plush material. The tables looked like they were hand carved from actual pine wood and had a glossy finish. The lighting in the room was warm, then they dimmed the lights a bit just before we took our seats.

"I've never eaten here before, what would you recommend?" I asked.

"Personally, I'd tell you to try the garlic butter shrimp and linguini. It's to die for."

"That's one of my favorite dishes, but everywhere I've gone seems to disappoint, except for an Italian restaurant my dad and I frequent."

"I can guarantee you'll never want to order it from anywhere else *ever* again."

"How are you two this evening? My name is Renee and I'll be taking care of you tonight. Can I start you off with some drinks?"

"Bring us two Patrón margaritas. We'll also have the fried shrimp and haddock appetizer sampler, with light tartar sauce," he ordered.

John and I hadn't known each other very long, but he was most certainly speaking my language.

"John, I am absolutely stuffed. That was delicious, but I'm sorry to say, this would be my second go-to restaurant for garlic butter shrimp."

"Damn, I thought for sure this would knock your other place out of the park."

"It was a nice attempt, but it fell just a bit short."

"That's okay, I'm sure I'll have another chance to wow you."

"Maybe. So tell me, what company are you interviewing at next?"

"A large firm somewhere in the downtown district. I don't want to give too much away; I believe it would be bad luck. If I get the job we can go out and celebrate afterward, deal?"

"Deal."

"Thank you for introducing me to this place, I'll definitely come here again."

"Good. Hey Sheila, the night is still young, would you like to come over my place?"

"Do you live far from here?"

"No, not at all."

I don't know what is was about him, but I trusted him. If he passed my test tonight, then I knew for sure I could keep him around for a while.

We pulled up in front of a stone duplex condo not too far from the restaurant. There was a set of stone steps and a metal railing leading up to the white front door. There was a bronze number seven engraved into the top of the door.

Once we were inside, I was actually shocked. There wasn't anything too flashy or fancy inside, just a normal wooden table set, a two-piece polyester couch, and a large flat screen TV. "Have a seat wherever you'd like, I'll be right back."

John disappeared into the other room as I found a spot on the longer couch. I turned the TV on and a gruesome story was on the news: two men had to be air lifted to Medical Mass Hospital when a gas line exploded at a construction site, severely burning their skin off. "Man, I'd hate to have to deal with that paperwork. Poor guys though," John said as he resurfaced from the back.

"I know, it almost reminded me of something that happened a few days ago. I almost thought it was going to be that story."

"Oh, well hopefully it's nothing you have to deal with directly, that would suck," he laughed.

"Right...it *would* suck."

John entered the kitchen area and grabbed a bottle out of the fridge. "I take it you're a Moscato girl, right?"

"Wouldn't have anything else," I said.

He popped the cork and poured the bubbly liquid into two large wine glasses, then handed one to me.

"To bright starts, and new beginnings," he said, as we clinked them together. I inhaled my wine and he quickly refilled my glass. As I started chugging back the second glass, my phone started violently vibrating in my purse. I looked at the screen and had two missed calls from my brother, Kieran. I didn't bother responding because I knew it couldn't have been anything *that* important.

I returned my gaze to John and he was staring at me with a huge smile on his face.

Three glasses of wine later, I was definitely feeling quite the buzz. I placed the stem back on the carpet in front of me and slid closer to John. I placed my hand on his thigh and his body reacted fairly quickly to my touch. "Sheila, what are you doing?"

"Testing you, think you can handle that John?"

I slid my hand further up his thigh and directly over his zipper. He tightly grasped my wrist and pushed my hand away. "Do you not want this, John?"

"Of course I do, but my place, my rules." He slid to his knees and crawled in front of me, rubbing his hand up and down my skirt. "I've been thinking about the treasures under here for a while."

He hiked up my skirt and I lifted my hips to allow the material to slide up around my waist. He ran his nose across the top of my thighs, and then spread my knees apart.

Gently kissing the inside of my thigh, he inhaled then continued his journey to my mound. He teased me with one finger, running it up and down the seam of my lace panties, torturing me. "Sheila, do I have permission to have my way with you?"

I wanted to yell 'Why the fuck are you asking me this? Just go for it, you tease', but I replied with a simple nod yes.

"Thank you." He grabbed the bottom of my panties and completely ripped them off. Rubbing his nose against my clit, I could feel the wetness building inside of me. He gave my clit one gentle kiss and that was all it took. He firmly assaulted it with his tongue.

I lost count of how many orgasms that man gave me before sliding a condom on and introducing me to his cock. I only caught a quick glimpse of it, but it was definitely one of the biggest I'd seen in a while.

He shoved my feet on both sides of his shoulders and pumped as hard and as fast as he could. Tears welled in my eyes from the intense pleasure. My nipples were hard as rocks and my body was completely hot to the touch. He placed his hand around my throat and I lost it. My body lost all control and seized as I came—*hard.*

Flashing a quick smile, he continued his conquest until he too let go. "Fuck Sheila, I've never come that hard before."

"Neither have I." My legs felt like dead weight and my clitoris was completely engorged and still throbbing from the intense orgasm. I had to give myself a minute to regroup.

A few moments passed and I was finally able to sit up. I stood and smoothed the leather material that was bunched around my waist back down. I asked John where the bathroom was and hurried in to collect myself. I took my purse in with me and touched up my makeup in the mirror. I re applied my red lipstick and blush to my cheeks. My hair was a complete mess, so I pulled it back in a high ponytail. It would definitely be a night to remember.

My phone was still continuously vibrating so I picked it up and had ten missed calls and two texts from my brother. *I really wish he would get a life. Big sis isn't always gonna be there to bail his ass out.*

I returned to the living room where John was sitting on the couch. "I have to go, but I'll definitely be in touch. Good luck on your interview tomorrow!"

"Sheila, wait!" he yelled as I slammed his front door shut.

Saying good bye for the first time after sex with someone I was unfamiliar with never got easier the more often it happened. For some reason, I felt a strong urge to leave after sex with John, and I didn't know why. It was like my mind knew something bad was going to happen and wanted me to leave as soon as possible.

Ryan and Liam were the only two exceptions where I never questioned wanting to be around them afterward. I felt right staying with them. I felt *safe*.

TWENTY-ONE

Out of curiosity, I tried to call Kieran back, but he didn't answer. I felt a bit of guilt for not answering my phone earlier, and hoped he was okay.

As I pulled up to my condo, I felt a weird sensation in my stomach. Anytime I felt that, I knew something bad had happened or was going to happen. I locked my car and walked up the steps. I put the key in the hole and noticed something red on the handle of my door. It looked like blood.

I opened the door in a hurry, locked it back, and ran to the kitchen sink to wash my hands. I tried to call Kieran one last time, but again there was no response. *Dammit K, where are you?*

After spraying bleach on the front door, I took a hot shower. I went into the living room in my pajamas and took care of some work on my laptop. I heard a loud thump outside my front door and it nearly scared the piss out of me. I looked out of the peep hole and what I discovered was horrible.

"Oh my god, Kieran!" I yelled, yanking the door open and charging down the stairs.

My brother was lying on my steps, bleeding profusely from his nose and mouth—*barely* clinging to life. "Who did this to you?" I screamed, but he didn't respond.

I placed his head back down on the steps gently and ran inside to grab my phone. I called the cops and they were at my house in seconds, although it felt like hours.

"Ma'am, do you know who might have done this to him?" the tall blonde officer asked.

"No, he'd been calling my cell phone all night, but I was busy. I finally came home and there was blood on the handle of my door."

"Blood? Did you wash it off?"

"Yes, I didn't want that shit on my door."

"Ma'am, please watch your tone."

"Listen, I don't have time for this…officer Jeffrey. I'm tired. My brother arrived on my steps nearly dead. I just want to get to the hospital and make sure he doesn't die tonight. So dust, black light, whatever the hell it is you need to do, go for it. Just lock my door when you're done."

I ran back inside to get my keys after I found out what hospital he was being transported to.

I flew to Mount Sinai Hospital and ran to the receptionist desk. "Excuse me, I'm looking for my brother, Kieran Quinn."

The nurse tapped the keys on the computer as fast as she could and looked at me with a puzzled look on her face. "I'm sorry miss, there is no one here by that name."

"What do you mean? I saw the ambulance pick him up in front of my eyes. I spoke with Officer Jeffrey."

"Ma'am no one new has arrived here in the past hour."

Where the hell could my brother be? Frantic, I called my dad for help. "Dad it's me. Kieran is in trouble!"

Two hours later, we finally found my brother. Mount Sinai was full, and he had been rerouted to Memorial Hospital.

"Sheila, do you know who could have done this?" asked Dad.

"No, Dad. I have no clue. He had called me several times, but I ignored it, thinking he was up to his normal shenanigans."

"Oh, Sheila. You should have answered and made sure."

"Dad I know. I usually do, and it's normally nothing."

"Well obviously this time it was something, Sheila!"

I could see the fury burning in my dad's eyes. One thing we always promised each other as a family was to be there for one another no matter what. Apparently my one screw up may have cost my baby brother his life.

I looked over at my brother's body; he looked so calm, so peaceful. His dark hair was slicked straight behind his head, his eyes had black and blue rings surrounding them, and he had a huge gash on his upper lip. It tore me up inside to see him like this, whether he deserved it or not.

I grabbed his hand and squeezed it as tight as I could, hoping he'd wake up, but he didn't.

A brunette woman in a long white lab coat came into the room, and that feeling in the pit of my stomach returned. "Hi, I'm Dr. Lazario. Are you Kieran's father and sister?"

"Yes," we answered simultaneously.

"Kieran is one lucky guy, all things considered. He didn't have any broken bones, but the MRI did show that he had a brain hemorrhage. Do you know what kind of drugs he's on?"

"He was recently addicted to both cocaine and heroin," I responded.

"I see. Well his toxicology reports haven't come back yet, but by the small bruises and puncture wounds on his arms, I could have easily guessed heroin."

"So do you believe he over dosed?" Dad questioned.

"Yes, I'm just not exactly sure if he'll wake up or not tonight, though. There didn't seem to be a lot of damage in his brain, so with modern medicine he may just pull through."

"Thank you doc, please keep us informed," Dad replied.

"As soon as I receive the results, you'll be the first to know," she responded, then exited the room.

The tension in the air was thick between my father and me. He didn't say another word to me. I picked up my phone and noticed I'd never read the texts my brother had sent me.

Keiran (1): Eila, I'm in trouble.

Keiran (2): Please, r u home?

Keiran (3): Everything is getting dark, they're after me...help!

Dammit Keiran, what did you get yourself into?

TWENTY-TWO

Dad and I stayed the entire night at the hospital with my brother. He tested positive for both coke and heroin, which wasn't a huge surprise to say the least. He was still in a coma, but seemed stable otherwise.

I had to get back to the office, so Dad told me he'd stay behind and keep me updated on Kieran's condition.

I stopped by the local coffee shop after I ran home and changed out of my pajamas. I ordered the largest cup of coffee I could, with a double shot of espresso. I knew the weak coffee at the office wouldn't get me through the day.

"Sheila, are you all right? You look like crap," Ryan said.

"No, my stupid brother is in a coma."

"I'm sorry to hear that. What happened to him?"

"Drugs. The usual."

"Wow. Well if you need anything, let me know."

"I will, Ryan. Right now, I need to focus on Quinn National; my dad can handle my brother."

I sat at my desk and stared at my computer. I had no desire to work on anything, but I had to force myself to be productive. I checked my email and had a message from my lawyer.

FROM: LAWRENCE SHUMAN

SUBJECT: URGENT

SHEILA,

I'VE GOT GOOD NEWS AND SOME BAD NEWS. THE GOOD
NEWS IS NEITHER OF THE INJURED EMPLOYEES IS SUING
YOU DIRECTLY. THEY ARE BOTH CLAIMING WORKMAN'S
COMP SO THEY CAN GET PAID FOR THEIR LEAVE. I NEED
YOU TO FILL OUT AND SIGN THE DOCUMENTS ATTACHED
TO THIS EMAIL AND FAX THEM BACK TO ME AS SOON AS
POSSIBLE. IF WE DON'T GET THEM SOME MONEY SOON,
I'M AFRAID WE WILL GET SUED.

THE BAD NEWS IS THE COMPANY'S INSURANCE PREMIUM
WILL NOW GO THROUGH THE ROOF. WE NEED TO MAKE
SURE OUR ASSES ARE COVERED, AND ALSO TRY NOT TO
LET SOMETHING LIKE THIS HAPPEN AGAIN.

TAKE CARE,

-LAWRENCE

Great! Good news all around today. Fuck I need a drink.

I texted John to meet me at Sam's so we both could unwind. He told
me that his day hadn't gone so well either.

"So Sheila, what's going on?"

"My stupid brother is in a coma. I'm almost certain he mixed some shit together that he wasn't supposed to, fucked with the wrong people, and got his ass knocked out."

"Ouch. Sorry to hear that," he responded, placing the full beer bottle up to his lips.

"Yeah. So what's your bad news?"

"I didn't get the position, which sucks. I would have made some decent money at this place."

"That sucks. Do you have any more interviews this week?"

"Tomorrow, actually," he said with a hopeful tone.

"That's great news," I said, taking a sip of my dry martini.

"Yeah, I heard the boss is a real hard ass, but I hope to charm them."

"You'll be fine. Hey, let's get out of here," I said, chugging the last sip of my drink.

"Hello?" I said, after slipping my bra straps back over my shoulder as I placed my phone on speaker.

"Sheila, its Dad. Kieran is awake, come quickly."

If only you knew Dad.

"I'll be right there."

"Everything okay?" John questioned from the opposite side of his bed, with his sheet barely covering his lap.

"Well my brother's awakened from his coma, as I'm sure you heard."

"That's great!"

"Thanks. Well good luck with your interview tomorrow. Hopefully this job is promising for you."

"Thanks."

After redressing myself, I grabbed my purse and ran out the door.

I walked into my brother's hospital room and his eyes lit up once he saw my face. "E-E-Eila," he stuttered. He was trying so hard to speak but the connection between his brain and his lips wasn't quite functioning properly yet.

I walked over to him and gave him a hug. Even though he was a royal pain in my ass, I was happy that he was awake. "Kieran, I'm sorry."

"No, not fault."

Tears welled in my eyes as I stared into his. Truth be told, I still felt like complete shit for ignoring his calls. He could have died and I would've felt like an ever bigger jackass if he went missing and never returned.

It was extremely difficult for him to speak, which I knew must have been one of the effects from the brain damage the doctor told us about.

"Sheila, he'll have a long road to recovery, but at least he's awake and is still with us," Dad said from behind me.

"I know, but—"

"Stop. It's not your fault."

I turned around and looked at my father. His brown eyes bore into mine and I tried my best to listen to what he said, but it didn't stop the fact that I was still beating myself up on the inside.

The doctor came in to speak with us and told us that they wanted to run a few more tests on Kieran. Now that he was awake, they needed to assess the damage again. "We'll take good care of him," she said as a team of nurses came in after her. They brought in a smaller gurney to transport my brother on.

"Dad, I'm gonna go. Please keep me updated."

"I will, sweetheart."

TWENTY-THREE

As I prepared for the day's interviews, I knew I had to put Kieran in the back of my mind and stay focused. I didn't need that distraction. I couldn't let Quinn National go down in flames over the remorse and regret I felt deep down inside.

"Ms. Quinn, your ten o'clock is here to see you," Karen said over the intercom.

"Thank you, Karen. Send him in."

I had forgotten to pull out my sheet of questions that I normally asked people out of the bottom drawer of my desk. They were unique and slightly disturbing questions that I asked people who applied for a higher position in the company. It kept them guessing and on their toes.

I opened the drawer and found the paper as the gentleman walked into my office. "Just give me a sec."

After I fished it out of my desk and was about to make eye contact, a familiar voice spoke my name. "Sheila?"

I quickly returned my gaze to the doorway and John was standing in it.

You have got to be shitting me.

"Have a seat, John. Let's not make this weird, let's just keep this professional. A high paying position is on the line."

He sat down in front of me in his crisp all black suit and nodded in agreement.

"Name?" I asked.

"Jonathan Keegan."

"Why do you want to work here, John?"

"Honestly, because I feel I have something new and exciting to offer Quinn National."

"Such as?" I retorted, intrigued.

"Well for instance, I know there is no marketing director here. I have extensive business knowledge and a background in programming."

"Okay, and what does that mean?"

"It means I can help develop apps for your company. I know you've recently acquired a natural gas division and I believe I can effectively market it for you. I can create an app that will allow users with any smart phone to view their usage, compare potential usage with other companies, and compare previous usage before the conversion. It will also be able to track new sign ups and send us an instant feed when someone requests more information."

I honestly hadn't pegged him as a tech nerd and I also hadn't thought he'd come in here ready to offer something that would be so useful to the company. I figured this was going to be a breeze but it was not, and he'd definitely gotten my attention. I did need serious help with my Nat-Co department and this might be a step in the right direction.

"Next question. If for some reason I was at an inspection site and a drilling crane fell down on my head, instantly killing me, how would you deal with your new responsibility in the company? Also, how would you prevent that from happening in the first place?"

"Well for starters, you would not be allowed to be that close to the equipment. If for some reason you were in a freak accident, I'd assume leadership by hiring an assistant to handle the marketing while I would bring fresh ideas and market revenue to your company by keeping up with the latest trends and developing my own. I would also keep in touch with your family for advice before I'd make any company changes."

He knew how important my family was to me, even though he didn't know much about them. Those were things I needed to hear. I'd also done a thorough background check on him: he was a valued employee at his previous employer, but budget cuts did not allow him to progress any further.

"Okay, well thank you for your time. We will be in touch if we decide to proceed with hiring you for this company," I said with a stern look on my face as I shook his hand.

"Sheila, wait," he said with a genuine look of concern on his face.

"What?"

"I had no idea that you worked here. I hope you believe that."

"Okay, you can leave my office now, John. I have several more of these today."

As John exited the room, Ryan stepped in. "He looks like your type. Did you hire him?"

"And what exactly is my 'type', Ryan?"

"Attractive, smart, you know, the basics?"

"Haha very funny. He does have potential though, I won't deny that."

"Good, we need more men around this place anyway."

After sitting through five long and boring interviews, it was finally time to go home. I was only interested in two potential hires, John and another guy named Frank Dugan. Everyone else was either boring or lacking the real enthusiasm and creativity we needed. I needed new and fresh, not old and boring.

I pulled up in front of my condo and went straight into the bathroom upon entering. I threw some soaking salts into the tub before running the hot water and lit some vanilla scented candles to help me relax. I headed into the kitchen to see what wine selections I had left to enjoy with my bath.

After the tub was full, I stripped down and slid my foot into the water first to make sure it wasn't too hot. I placed my phone down beside the tub and poured a glass of pink Moscato before fully submerging myself into the water.

I could feel the stress of the day leaving my body as I sank further into the soapy water, but my mind started racing a mile a minute.

Last night, I slept with John. Today, I interviewed Jonathan Keegan for the vacant Vice President position at my job. My life had been like one huge rollercoaster, and I had my hands high in the sky without a care in the fucking world.

I felt warmth grow between my legs just thinking about John and rubbed my hand against my throbbing clit, trying to relive the tender moment we'd shared the previous night: his toned body on top of mine, our hips grinding together as we both came to climax. I was still a tad sore from the experience, but I knew I had to have more of him.

TWENTY-FOUR

Rose and Karen entered my office in the morning, asking me about the interviews from the day before. They wanted to know if any of them would be hired. I told them that unfortunately, I had to run my top picks by Roger before I could make a final decision, which I dreaded.

"Hey Roger, could you come into my office please? We need to have a discussion," I said over his intercom.

"I'll be right in, Sheila."

Roger was in his late fifties with a clean-shaven head, a gray and black beard, and dark freckles across his cheeks. He was very tall and husky built with olive skin.

"Close the door and have a seat. We need to discuss the potential hires I interviewed yesterday."

After hours of deliberating and providing him with valid points, we finally came to a decision. We decided to hire them both.

I let Roger call them both and deliver the news. I needed to get back to the hospital to check on my brother.

I grabbed two coffees from the hospital lobby and headed up to my brother's room. As I rounded the corner, I saw the staff rushing a body on a gurney down the hall and my heart fell into the pit of my stomach.

I saw Dr. Lazario and my world started to shatter. I rushed into the room to find an empty bed and my dad kneeling in front of it, praying. "Dad, please talk to me."

I dropped the coffee on the floor and ran over to him, trying to bring him to his feet. "Dad?"

"Your brother had a grand mal seizure, Sheila. There's a slim chance he might not make it."

My eyes erupted with tears. They stung my face as they slid down my cheeks. I punched the bed in frustration. *No! You've got to pull it together, Sheila. He will be okay, have faith!*

I quickly wiped the tears away from my face and sat down on the bed. *Have faith.*

Dad and I stayed at the hospital all night, waiting for someone to come back with an answer. Finally at six a.m. we received some news.

"Mr. Quinn, we were able to stabilize Kieran, but he did lose a lot of oxygen. I'm afraid there may have been further damage to his brain."

I stared at the doctor blankly, trying to make sense of everything. He was only twenty-five years old, he didn't deserve this. He didn't deserve to fight for his life so suddenly. He wasn't an awful person, he just got mixed up with the wrong group of assholes.

"Why isn't Shannon here, Dad?"

"Because you know your sister isn't as strong as us. She'd be in here causing a serious commotion. Once he's fully stable, I'll inform her."

On my drive home, my phone rang. I didn't bother looking at the ID and hit the Bluetooth in my ear. "Hello?"

"There's the strange voice I haven't heard in ages."

"Liam?"

"Yeah, what's wrong? You sound upset?"

"Kieran is in the hospital."

"Is he okay?" he said with a genuinely concerned tone.

"No, but I don't wanna talk about it right now."

"Okay. What do you want to talk about?"

"I don't *want* to talk at all," I retorted.

"I'll be at your place in ten, Sheila. Please let me in when I get there."

"Whatever, Liam," I sighed.

I went inside my condo and headed straight for the fridge. I had a full bottle of tequila and no work tomorrow. I planned on drinking it until I couldn't properly form coherent sentences.

Countless shots later, I heard a knock on the door. I staggered over to it and unlocked it. "Hey, you! Come on in," I slurred.

"Sheila, how many drinks have you had?" Liam questioned.

"Does it really matter?" I said falling into his arms. "Scuse me."

He gently ran his fingers over my cheek, pushing my hair behind my ear. "Quinn, I know how much your family means to you, but you don't have to drink your sorrows away. You're better than this."

"I know—but it's my fault, I didn't answer his call."

"It is not your fault your brother is a drug addict. You could only bail him out and cover his ass but so many times. I know it hurts, but he'll be okay. Every single one of you Quinns are fighters."

The way the lights shone on Liam's gray eyes made him look so irresistible.

I poured myself one more shot, downed it, and pushed him back on my couch. After quickly mounting him, I ripped my top off. "Please make me forget, Liam, just for tonight."

TWENTY-FIVE

I was awakened by a loud pounding on my front door. I looked over at the clock on the cable box and it was five a.m. *Who in the hell?*

I looked over and Liam was passed out on the love seat. I wrapped the blanket from the couch around my naked body and looked through the peephole.

Fuck, it's Ryan. I glanced over at the couch once more and Liam hadn't budged. I cracked the door open. "What?" I whispered.

"Uh, aren't you forgetting something?"

I stared hard at Ryan: he was in his workout gear. "Can you give me like an hour and I'll be ready?"

"Sure, let me in."

"I can't right now. I'll meet you at the reservoir, okay?" I slammed the door shut in his face.

I ran into the back and grabbed my running gear out of the laundry room, then ran into the bathroom to wash the shame and stench of alcohol off of me.

After I got out of the shower, I tossed my gear on, sent Liam home, and ran down to the reservoir to meet Ryan.

"I'm sorry. I had a bad night."

"I'll say. You reeked of booze when you answered the door. What's been going on with you, Sheila?"

"What do you mean?" I asked, playing stupid.

"You've been distant. The last few days you've been *different*. You hardly even speak to me, and you almost forgot the running date that *you* made today."

"Look, I don't know what you think we had, but there is *nothing* going on between us. I had a few vulnerable moments with you, but nothing else. I'm only human and I make plenty of fucking mistakes!"

He walked over to me and placed his hand behind my neck. "You don't mean that, Sheila. What I felt was genuine, and don't you *dare* tell me it was *nothing*."

I could see the hurt in his dull blue eyes. *What the fuck are you getting yourself into, Sheila?*

"Let's just run okay? Run until we can barely stand. See you in two hours," I said, breaking his hold and slipping my headphones into my ears.

I ran and ran until it became difficult to continue. I sat down on a nearby bench to rest and give my muscles a good stretching. I wasn't prepared for the run at all, but I damn sure needed it. It helped me clear my mind and also helped me shed some of the emotion I felt deep within my soul.

Ryan ran up and sat down beside me on the bench. "You were in the zone, Sheila. I swore I blinked and you were miles down the road."

"I had a lot on my mind, I guess."

"Wanna go and grab a bite to eat?" he asked, extending his hand toward mine.

"No thanks, I'm gonna run a few more miles."

"Need any company?"

"Ryan, go home. I'll be fine. I need to clear my mind anyway."

Ryan, upset, turned around and ran back in the direction we'd just come from, while I got up to run a few laps around the reservoir.

After two full laps around the large body of water, I sat down on a patch of grass in front of it. I looked at my reflection in the water and I didn't like the image I saw looking back at me through the flowing current.

I'd let my brother's health issues take me to a dark place that I didn't want to be. I'd let myself become weak and naïve, two things I prided myself on not being.

I ran my hand over the top of my hair, smoothing a few stray hairs back with it. *Life will always be full of unfinished roads, but it's up to you to pave the perfect path to fulfill your destiny.* It was a quote my mom had said to me when I was younger, but now that I was older it made a lot more sense.

I looked at my watch: it was almost noon, and I was starving.

After devouring my food and catching a quick shower, I grabbed my phone and had several messages from Liam, Ryan, and John asking me the same damn question: *Where are you?*

Frankly, it was none of their damn businesses, but since it was Saturday night, I decided one of them should take me out on a date.

TWENTY-SIX

"John, thanks for meeting me."

"Sheila, wow. You look gorgeous."

I was wearing a skin-tight black and red asymmetrical dress and black pumps. Waved dark curls bounced on my shoulders and down my back. I'd decorated my lips with my favorite red lipstick and painted my eyes with smoky eye shadow, making my hazel eyes pop.

"Thanks," I responded, clutching my purse close to my hip.

"Sheila," he said extending his arm toward mine. "Let's make our grand entrance, shall we?" We walked into Club Black Widow, the hottest night club just outside of Boston.

Neon lights swirled around the dark fog filled room. The DJ was in front of the dance floor on a stage with huge bass extenders and speakers. An up-tempo remix of "Toxic" by Britney Spears started playing and the drunken crowd went nuts, shaking their rhythm-less nonexistent asses.

John left my side briefly to grab us a few drinks, and as soon as he broke his hold on my arm, I felt like he set off some kind of desperate horny asshole homing beacon. "Excuse me miss, care to dance?" a tall bald gentleman asked.

"No thanks."

"Well if you change your mind, come find me."

Several others approached me and were all shot down. *Dammit John, where the hell are you?*

There was a soft tap on my shoulder and I rolled my eyes as I turned around to face another potential let down. "Here you go," John said, handing me a margarita.

"Christ, it's about time!" I yelled over the song. "I swear ten assholes approached me the second you left my side."

"Well," he said scanning my body from head to toe, "I can't blame them for trying."

The club was so live. I danced until I felt every single curl leave my head. John kept pumping me with drinks until I finally stopped him and asked to get some food before the kitchen closed in an hour.

We split a half-pound turkey burger and fry basket before we left.

I had pre-booked a hotel nearby to crash at for the night. I knew I was going to get drunk and didn't want to risk driving home intoxicated. John followed me to the door of my room and kissed me good night.

I went into the bathroom and cleaned the makeup off my face with the makeup removing scrubbing wipes I had in my purse.

I walked back into the room and kicked my heels off before sitting down on the edge of the queen sized bed. Looking at my reflection in the mirror on the dresser, I pulled the zipper down the side of my dress.

A knock at the door interrupted me before I could pull the dress off. "Hello?" I said, walking toward the door and clutching the side of my dress so it wouldn't fall. I looked through the peep hole and John was standing in front of my door. As I opened it, he pushed his way in, squeezing me tightly in his arms.

With a deep intensity in his eyes, I could tell he wanted to devour me. The door shut behind him, startling me as he walked me over to the bed. I was ready to give him anything he wanted.

"Sheila—" I forcefully pressed my lips against his, silencing any doubt he had in his mind.

He unzipped the last part of my dress and it fell to the floor, revealing my red lingerie set. Placing his hand in the arch of my back, he traced his tongue on the side of my neck. His hand slid up my back, unsnapping my bra clasps and letting my breasts fall free.

He spun me around so I could see myself in the mirror as he gently slid one finger underneath the seam of my panties. He rubbed my clit and cupped my breast with his free hand. "I want you to come on my fingers, Sheila. I want you to keep your eyes open while you do, so you can see how beautiful you look as you succumb to me."

Heat rose from deep down inside of me as John's fingers picked up the pace. My nipples hardened and my head flew back on his shoulders as he dipped his fingers into my core. "Look into the mirror, Sheila. Don't close your eyes," he whispered into my ear as I felt myself letting go.

His cock pressed up against me and it was my turn to return the favor.

TWENTY-SEVEN

Monday—*sweet, sweet, Monday*. It was the shittiest day of the week for most, but I always looked forward to it.

Today was John and Frank's first day as Vice President of Marketing and Vice President of Telecommunications, two jobs that I knew would suit them both well.

They both had to deal with Roger while I tackled the new permits for a secondary building for Nat-Co.

I walked into the parking garage elevator and went up to my suite. As the doors opened I smiled at Rose. "Morning."

"Morning Ms. Quinn, you look well rested and refreshed. "

I spent the weekend in a hotel fucking one of the new VPs, of course I looked refreshed.

I walked into my office and hung my trench coat on the rack, then placed my briefcase on top of my desk.

"Morning Ms. Quinn, here's your coffee."

"Thank you, Ryan." He stood in front of my desk smiling at me.

"What?"

"Nothing, you just look—happy."

"I am Ryan. I got rid of the old pathetic Sheila and brought back stone cold Sheila."

"Good for you. Oh and 'Stone Cold', you might want to check your email. If you need anything stronger than that coffee after you read it, like vodka, let me know."

What the hell does that mean? Why would I need vodka at eight thirty in the morning?

"That son of a bitch!" I yelled at my screen. "He has no idea who he is fucking with. He wants to play hard ball? Then we'll play hard ball."

Keith Lee was kind enough to get a lien put on the building I wanted across the street. The email wasn't actually from him, but from the bank. I knew he was behind it though; it was too damn coincidental.

I spent most of the morning searching online for dirt on Keith. There had to be something. Marital issues, a teen pregnancy, something, anything I could use to blackmail him into leaving me the hell alone.

Search after search, and nothing came up. This man was good at covering his tracks, but I had a secret weapon for situations like this. There was one man I could call to take care of this, and his name was Lucky.

"Hey Lucky, it's Sheila. I need a favor; can you meet up for lunch today?"

"Anything for you Ms. Quinn," he responded.

"Hey Ryan, I'm gonna step out for lunch. I'll be back in about an hour." I locked up my office and headed to the diner on Oak Street.

Lucky was standing in front of the diner with his infamous black hooded sweat shirt with a white skull on the front. His black backpack was slung over his shoulder and a metal chain hung from his denim jeans.

"Hey Lucky," I said stepping out of my car.

"Oh my god, Sheila, you look amazing," he said giving me a hug.

"You don't look too bad yourself. You filled in a lot."

"Two years clean. I hit the gym now for my fix instead of drugs; I had to leave those alone."

"God, if only Kieran was as smart as you."

"How is he by the way?"

"Not good, but we'll talk about him later."

Lucky was an old friend of my brother's. We'd hooked up once years ago after I saved his mom's home from foreclosure. He couldn't afford to pay me back so he promised to be my clean up man. He could get dirt on anyone or make them disappear if needed.

"Let me grab a gyro and we can get to work. Would you like one, Sheila?"

"Of course."

We found a quiet spot at the dog park around the corner from the diner to talk. No one would bother us there.

Lucky had gotten pretty attractive over the years, but he had one *flaw* that he always pointed out: a scar across his eye, which I honestly thought made him look badass. It stretched from his forehead to the top of his cheek, the result of a freak incident during one of his drug binges.

His chocolate brown eyes cut over at me as he took a bite of his wrap. His face was clean-shaven and I could see the dark brown hair creeping from underneath his hood. "So what do you need to know, Lucky?"

"His name and where he works should be all the info I need," he responded, placing his sandwich back down on the foil it had come in and pulling his laptop out of his bag.

I pulled out the copy of Keith's license I'd taken from him the night in the hotel. "Is this good enough?"

"It's perfect. Give me a few minutes and I can hack into any electronic thing that he owns. His phone, computer, GPS, anything!"

"Dig for anything and everything you can see," I said, taking a bite out of my wrap.

After ferociously typing away at his laptop for what seemed like forever, he turned his laptop around to show me what he'd found. A bunch of coded nonsense that I couldn't understand was on his screen. It literally looked like something straight out of the movie "The Matrix".

"What does all of that mean?"

"It means I have enough dirt on this asshole to send him packing."

"Excellent."

Now that that was done, then came the hard part. How the hell was I going to get close enough to Keith to nail his ass to the coffin?

TWENTY-EIGHT

Keith was actually pretty eager to see me again, so eager it was almost fucking sickening. It almost seemed as if he had forgotten about the whole me abandoning him in the hotel incident.

I met up with him at another seafood restaurant named The Shack.

"Sheila, I accept your apology. I know that was just an honest mistake that you are willing to make up to me, right?" he said, touching the top of my hand.

We were seated fairly quickly and placed our orders with the waitress. "So Keith, why is there a lien on the property you gave me the permit for?"

"Well *technically* Sheila, you stole the permit information from me."

"Well *technically* Keith, you're an asshole."

He smiled at me as he took a sip of his water. "You're correct."

I tried my best to ease into things as gradually as I possibly could, but he was making it very difficult.

After our meal Keith suggested going to another hotel nearby. *I swear this dude is a complete idiot.*

"Keith, wait. I have an even better idea."

"And what is that?" he asked with a puzzled look on his face.

"One sec." I pulled a manila folder out of my briefcase and slid it across the table to him.

"What's this?"

"Take a look inside."

It took less than a minute for his entire facial expression to change. "Where the fuck did you get these? I thought I had this taken care of."

"Well I guess your clean up person didn't do a very good job, now did they?"

Inside the folder were photos of Keith snorting drugs off a male hooker's ass cheek in the back of a limo. Also inside were photos of his wife June, and his three kids, Zach, Amy, and Preston.

"Now, I could leak the first photo to the press and your precious high class family would be ruined."

"No, please. I'll do anything you want."

"Good, take that fucking lien off of my property and leave me and everyone else at Quinn National the fuck alone."

"Deal, I'll take care of everything first thing in the morning."

"Good. You can keep the folder."

He hysterically started laughing. "You stupid bitch. Why would you give me these? Now I don't have to do shit you say!"

"Is that so?" I pulled out my cell phone and played him a video I had in my archives. It was of him in the same limo with the hooker, only he was sucking his dick and I had a clear view of the whole thing. The color faded from his skin and his green eyes looked dull. I got up, patted him on the shoulder, and said goodbye, leaving him high and dry in the middle of the restaurant.

In a matter of hours, I was able to get everything I needed taken care of, all before heading back into the office.

"What did you do?" Ryan questioned.

"What do you mean?"

"You have that devious grin on your face. You only smile like that when you've either exacted revenge on someone or you've closed an important deal."

Damn this kid knows me too well. There was no need to lie to him, per se, but I didn't have to tell him every detail either. "Let's just say, tomorrow the lien will be gone and we won't have any more issues with the bank again."

"You didn't do anything illegal, did you?"

"I'll never tell, Ryan."

"Fine, you're so damn stubborn."

"Yes she is," John interrupted.

Ryan looked over at me and quickly excused himself from my office, closing the door behind him.

"John! How's your first day at Quinn National so far?"

"It's going I guess. I had hoped to learn the ropes from you, not Roger. Does that guy have a permanent stick up his ass or something?"

"He sure does," I laughed.

"Great, and I'll be stuck with him all week."

"Sorry, but all new hires have to train with him before you can even step foot in my office. So, consider yourself privileged to be in here right now, Mr. Keegan."

"I feel more than privileged, Sheila. What are you doing tonight?"

"I hadn't given it much thought. I'll probably go and visit Kieran, then go home afterward."

"Oh, I wanted to take you out to dinner, but I guess it'll have to wait for another time."

"Yeah, this week isn't a good week for me."

"Okay, well I should be going. I'm sure I'll be seeing you around."

"Yes, I'll be here."

TWENTY-NINE

Ryan, John, and Liam all offered to take me out, but I didn't feel like being bothered with any of them.

As I lay in my bed, alone and disconnected from the world, I realized I had almost everything I'd ever wanted right in front of me.

I was one of the youngest CEOs in the country. I could have any man I wanted, yet I felt like something was missing. For the first time in my life, I was confused. I wasn't confused about where I was going in life, nor my goals. I was confused about which man truly deserved my time. I had made the stupid mistake of getting close to three of them. It usually came naturally for me to keep my heart quiet, but for some reason, it now felt the need to express how it felt. Only, it was just as confused as me and didn't know who deserved it.

Oh what the hell. I sat up, looked at the clock, and saw that it was only ten p.m. I was hardly ever alone at that time; I usually had some sort of company with me or I was out. I picked up my phone and responded to his text.

Me: Hope you're still willing to take me out, I'll see you in 30.

"Well aren't you a sight for sore eyes," Ryan joked.

"I know, I know. It's been a while. I've had a lot going on."

"Sure…You've had a lot of *someone* going on," he laughed.

"Whatever. So are you buying me a drink or what?"

"Bartender, two shots please," he ordered.

"Anything in particular?" the bartender questioned.

"Surprise us, we can handle just about anything," Ryan answered, winking at me for confirmation.

As we waited for our drinks, I stared at Ryan as he watched the game on TV. He was wearing a pair of dark wash jeans and a plaid button up shirt. Since it was a last minute get together, I'd thrown on my favorite tan blazer—the one that barely covered my lace bra—over a pair of black skinny jeans and heels.

"So Sheila, what the hell was the lien about? As long as Quinn National has been around, I've never seen a lien in any of the previous paperwork you provided me with to scan."

"Remember that night I faxed all of that shit to the office, around midnight?"

"Yeah," he said, signaling the bartender to bring us a few beers.

"That asshole had something to do with it, so I had him taken care of."

"Sheila, please tell me you didn't kill the man."

"What if I did?" I smirked.

"Then I better hurry up and put some money aside for bail."

"I didn't have him killed, but you should still have the money set aside anyway. You know, just in case?"

We hung out at the bar until almost closing time. I drank the last sip of my beer and ran to the ladies room.

As I washed my hands, I overheard people fucking in the last stall and I had to admit, it turned me on a little.

"What's with the smile on your face?" Ryan questioned as I walked out of the bathroom door.

"Someone is getting nailed in the bathroom. No big deal."

"Oh…well, uh, what are your plans now?" I heard the nervous tremble in his voice.

"I'm heading home, Ryan. But it was nice to hang out and catch up. I missed this."

"Me too. Sheila?"

"Yes?"

"Be careful."

"Of what?" I questioned.

"John. I don't trust him."

"And why not?"

"I feel like he just came out of nowhere and there's just something *off* about him."

"You're just being paranoid. Good night, Ryan."

I thought it was cute that Ryan was looking out for me like that, but I was a big girl and could fight my own battles. If I felt John was a no good piece of shit, he'd be fired on the spot.

THIRTY

"So how's the app coming along, John?"

He turned around, startled by the sound of my voice. "Good, I was just uh, doing some research. There's some coding I'm having a bit of trouble with."

"Okay, well let me know if you need anything."

"Will do, boss."

I went to check on Frank to see if his pitch was ready. We needed to draw more investors into our natural gas division; the more people we got involved, the more revenue we would earn.

He'd also come up with the brilliant idea to get the local electric company to merge with us to help lower the consumer costs for the service.

"Everything is running smoothly. I'll be sitting down in two meetings tomorrow, so fingers crossed." Frank confirmed.

Frank was a pretty confident guy. He was bald with a thick goatee that wrapped around his lips and had a solid frame.

I walked back down the hallway and stopped in front of Ryan's office. He looked up at me from his desk, shooting me a flirtatious smile before I returned to my office.

I sat down at my desk and heard a commotion down the hall. "Karen?" I said over the intercom. "What's going on down there?"

"Shannon is here," she replied.

Fuck...

"Sheila! Why didn't you tell me about my brother?"

"*Your* brother? Since when was he just *your* brother? You could care less about him."

"I care more about him then you know."

"Sure."

She dropped her thousand-dollar Coach bag on the floor and sat down in front of my desk. Her golden dyed blonde locks were curled to perfection. She ripped her expensive shades off her face and gave me an evil glare.

Although she always pissed me off, she was gorgeous. Everything about her appearance was flawless. She was tall and naturally thin, with perfect breasts and money green eyes.

"What did you really come here for, Shannon?"

"I feel so out of touch with everyone. I feel like I'm losing you all. When Dad was admitted to the hospital all he talked about was *you*. I sat right in front of him for days, and all he cared about was 'his Sheila'. Now Kieran is in a medically induced coma and the only way I found out was because I had to pry it out of Dad. I hate feeling like such an outcast, sis."

"Shannon, let's be honest here for a sec. You're the one that distanced yourself from us. You turned down the internship here, and although you went to college, what are you doing with your business management degree? *Nothing.* Maybe this was the reality check you so desperately needed."

"Knock, knock. So sorry to interrupt, Ms. Quinn, but you are needed downstairs; I'm having a *problem* with my app," John interrupted.

"Are we done here, Shannon?"

"I guess, go run your stupid company," she said, rolling her eyes. She slid her glasses back on her face and snatched her purse off the floor before storming out of my office.

"So, what's going on, John?"

"Nothing...I could hear her giving you shit all the way down the hall and figured you needed a way to get rid of her."

"You were right, thanks for that."

"You're welcome. So are you free to go out with me yet? We both could really use a nice seafood dinner," he asked, flashing me a devilish grin.

"Sure, but this time, we go to one of my favorite places."

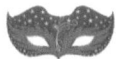

I asked John to meet me at the Sotto Italia restaurant. It was my second go-to place to get great seafood. I wasn't ready to bring him to my number one place just yet; I still didn't know him that well.

It was a chilly fall evening so I wore my navy blue pant suit with black pumps and wore my hair in a loose side ponytail.

John met me at the door wearing a long tailored suit jacket with matching pants. "Ladies first," he said as he opened the door for me.

"What a true gentleman."

It was pretty slow for a Tuesday night and we were seated immediately.

Our waiter's name was Jason and he was absolutely gorgeous. Short blonde hair, a strong chiseled chin, and I could see the indentions of his muscles underneath his formal fitted uniform.

The way he said 'I'll take care of you' as he took our order made my insides tingle. If I had been there without John, I would have found out how well he really would take care of me.

"So John, tell me more about yourself."

"What would you like to know?"

"Do you have any siblings?"

"Yes, I have two brothers and one sister."

"Are they younger or older than you?"

"All of them are older than me."

"Aw, so you're the 'baby'. How was that growing up?"

"Well if you must know, it sucked."

The waiter came back with our drinks and a second waiter came behind him with our meals. "Enjoy."

"Thank you. Why is that, John?"

"I had the pleasure of receiving *everyone's* hand me downs."

"Ouch!" I laughed.

"Go ahead, laugh your ass off. It sucked *badly.*"

"I can imagine."

"So what about you, Sheila?" he paused. "How many siblings do you have?"

"Just the two: the hell-beast you met earlier, and my younger brother, Kieran."

"How's he doing by the way?"

"Not good, but I don't really wanna talk about it."

"I can respect that. The subject is dropped."

"How are you folks enjoying your meals tonight? the waiter interrupted.

"It's delicious. Thank you!" John snapped back.

I glanced over at John and as our eyes connected I felt a spark between us. There was definitely something there, but I had to keep my head and my legs together for now.

"Sheila, I must admit that place blows my favorite spot out of the water. Everything tasted, I don't know, fresher? Anyway, you have a good night. I'll see you at work tomorrow."

"Of course, night." John escorted me to my car to make sure I got in safely before he ran across the lot to find his own vehicle.

He was a really nice guy, but I had that off feeling in the pit of my stomach, again.

THIRTY-ONE

After dinner, I went straight to the hospital to visit my brother. Dad was still sitting at his bedside and I could tell he hadn't left in days by the facial hair that had grown. I didn't stay long, I just wanted to see him and see if there were any changes in brain activity. Thankfully, his brain was still active despite the damage it'd received from oxygen deprivation.

Dad gave me the third degree for not coming by all week, but it hurt to come by every day and see someone you care about like that. It almost reminded me of Mom before she passed. Kieran looked just like her, so it brought back horrible memories for me.

I promised Dad I'd try and visit twice a week, just to get him off my back.

All of the city permits I needed to start the Nat-Co division were signed and underground construction was set to start the next day.

Hopefully Frank could nail his two meetings, and that would get us a step in the right direction.

John was making a lot of progress on the Nat-Co app. He already had the user friendly design created on Illustrator and had implemented the logo I'd created for it. "John this looks amazing. I can't wait to see the app once it's up and running."

"It'll only take me another week or so to complete the design. The hard part is getting all the coding to work, bug free."

"Well you take as much time as you need. We hired you for a reason, so don't let the company down."

"I won't, Sheila. You can definitely count on me."

I received a phone call later that night, a call that had the ability to break me into a million tiny pieces. I'd known this day would come, but I'd been in denial. Not him, not us; my family couldn't handle another blow like this.

Kieran was brain dead. I didn't want to believe it and I couldn't bring myself *to* believe it. When my Dad called me, it was the furthest thing from my mind.

I sat on my bed frozen in place, staring blankly at the wall. I couldn't find any motivation to say or do anything, but if I learned anything from it, it was that life is too short.

I arrived at the hospital with tears falling from my eyes. I was hurting and I didn't care to hide it anymore. I took the elevator upstairs and slowly walked through the halls until I reached the room. I peered in and saw my father hovering over my brother's body. The ventilator that was keeping him alive was still on, but I could feel he was no longer with us.

"Dad, what do we do now?"

"He's gone Sheila. First, we pray, and then the final decision rests in your hands."

"What do you mean?"

"He only trusted one person with his power of attorney, Sheila."

"That should be you, right?"

"No...it's you."

"Me?" It was up to me to decide to pull the plug on my own brother. I guess he felt I would do the honorable thing and put him out of his misery if he were ever to be incapacitated.

It was an honor, but it also scared me. Did I end my twenty-five- year-old brother's life? Or did I pray for some sort of miracle?

I walked around the opposite side of the bed and grabbed his hand. His pulse was low and I could barely see him breathing. There was absolutely no way I could let him suffer, but I felt bad and wanted Shannon to get a chance to say good bye before I made my decision.

"Did you call Shannon, Dad?"

"Yes, she should be here any minute."

I squeezed my brother's hand, hoping he'd squeeze back...but there was nothing. Tears silently fell from my face and onto the sheet that was covering him. "Kieran, why? Why did you have to be so stupid?" I yelled, fighting the urge to place my hands around his throat.

"No! Is he really dead?" a voice shrieked from behind us.

Shannon ran into the room with her mascara running down her cheeks. She looked a mess but I knew I didn't look any better. She stood beside me and rubbed Kieran's leg. "Why? He's only twenty-five! He's a freaking baby for Christ's sake!" She inhaled deeply to calm herself down. "You had so much potential little brother. So what now, Dad? Are you going to pull the plug?" she questioned.

"No. It's out of my hands."

Shannon cut her eyes over at me. I could feel how hurt she was that I had all the power and she had none.

"Well, Sheila," she fake smiled. "What are you going to do?"

"Pull it. He shouldn't have to suffer any longer."

Shannon collapsed on the floor and completely lost it. She was always the over the top drama queen in the family.

I looked back at Kieran. It honestly looked like he was in a very deep sleep. His olive skin was still full of life. His long dark hair still had its shine and luster, and the hospital staff had done a great job keeping him clean-shaven.

As my dad bent down to console my sister, I went to find the doc to give her my decision.

I left the hospital and walked straight into the nearest pub. I didn't care about anything or anyone at that moment. I wanted to feel absolutely numb and drown the conflicting thoughts out of my head.

I sat down on an empty bar stool directly in front of the TV and ordered a double shot of whiskey. The bartended stared at me as I pounded both drinks back. "I'll have another double shot."

"I've never seen you in here before, but by the looks of those empty shot glasses I can tell you're trying to forget something."

"Listen, you're my bartender, not my therapist, so just keep the fucking drinks coming, 'kay?"

"Aw, a feisty one. Yes ma'am," he replied.

Six shots in and the pain was slowly starting to ease. All the yelling and the sound of clinking bottles were starting to amplify, but I couldn't understand anything.

"Sheila?" I heard from across the bar. I looked around to see where the voice had come from, but I couldn't spot anyone. I wrapped my fingers around the last shot in front of me and as I put the glass up to my lips, I heard it again, this time a lot closer. I chugged the shot back and that's when I saw him.

"Liam, what are you doing here?"

"Celebrating, you?"

"Trying to forget," I sighed.

"Forget what?" he said, tilting my chin up towards him.

"Killing my brother."

"Wait, what? Why would you be killing him?"

"Because his brain is dead, Liam, it's fucking dead!"

"What happened?"

"Drugs happened. Are you really that surprised?"

"No, I can't say that I am."

"And now I have to be the one to pull the plug on him."

"I see. But you don't want to yet?"

"No, I wanted to wait a few more days before I ended it. I don't want to see him suffer but the look of pain and sorrow on Dad and Shannon's faces made me wait. They needed a little more time to come to grips with his death and let go."

"Wow. I am so sorry. I remember how much your family meant to you," he said, gazing into my eyes.

I looked at him and it started happening again. I don't know what it was about those gray eyes of his, but they had the power to draw me in and make me feel.

"Let's get out of here, Sheila," he said slamming a hundred dollar bill down on the counter. "Keep the change, bar keep." He led me outside the bar and into his brand new Nissan. He opened the passenger side door and helped me with my seatbelt. My head was swimming and I felt like I was having an out-of-body experience.

The whole trip went by in one quick blur and before I knew it, he was opening my door again, escorting me out and up the stairs. I firmly gripped the banister so I wouldn't fall back down the stairs. Liam let out a low chuckle and put his arm around me to help keep me balanced.

He unlocked the door and walked me over to the couch. "Would you like some water?" he asked.

"No, bring me the strongest liquor you have in here."

"Sheila, are you okay?"

I ran my hand across my cheek, not realizing I'd been crying. "I just want to forget, Liam. Help me forget."

He walked into the kitchen and opened the cabinet above the stove. I heard glasses clinking, and then he placed two shot glasses down onto the counter. He grabbed a huge glass bottle with fancy engraving on the side and poured the amber liquid into both glasses.

He brought them both over to me and as I went to grab one he told me to wait. "I'll help you forget but I can't do that unless I forget too."

After a few drinks, Liam and I were standing in front of each other completely naked. I shoved him down onto the carpet, ready to have my way with him. His dick was hard as a rock as I climbed on top of it.

I rocked my hips back and forth, and then bounced up and down on it. The room started to spin and I felt myself losing control of my body. He clasped his hand around my neck and I looked down at him. "Ride this dick, Sheila. Don't you quit on me yet!"

I rode him so hard that I got rug burn on my knees, but it was well worth it to orgasm harder than I had in a long time.

THIRTY-TWO

I hadn't realized how bad I'd scuffed my knees until I saw them in the mirror as I got ready for work the next morning. I rubbed healing lotion on them and decided it was a pant suit kind of day.

Ryan would be the first to notice and I didn't need him *or* John breathing down my neck.

I brushed my hair into a smooth high ponytail and added a few curls to the end. I applied a fun vibrant shade of pink lipstick before heading out the door.

"So Frank, how did the meetings go?"

"Well Ms. Quinn, they went okay. I've managed to bring a few more investors on board, but the electric company wants to hear from you directly before they give a final answer."

"Did they say why?"

"Well, they said before they invest or merge with a huge production such as this, they needed to talk to the head of the company first."

"Fine, schedule a meeting with them next Monday," I huffed.

"Will do, is there anything else?"

"Yes, send in Mr. Keegan."

I sat down at the head of the conference table and waited for his arrival. Ryan snuck in and brought me a fresh cup of coffee while I waited. "You look great today, Ms. Quinn." He smiled before running back out of the room.

"Sheila, how goes it?"

"It's Ms. Quinn, asshole. Close the door behind you."

"Sorry, 'Ms. Quinn', my apologies. You summoned me?"

"Yes, John. Now have a seat." He sat down at the opposite end of the table with a look of confusion on his face.

"So John, I did do my homework before hiring you and I must say, I know you can usually produce a bug free app within a few weeks, am I correct?"

"Yes."

"So why are you taking your sweet ass time with this one? Do you think just because we slept together that I'd let you slack around at work?"

"Well, yes and no."

"Well unless your only purpose was to screw me and fuck over my company, you can walk out that door right now. Otherwise, you can get your ass in gear and get this app fixed and completed by the weekend. Do I make myself clear?"

"Yes…crystal in fact."

That strange feeling in my gut returned and warned me to keep my eyes on him. I really thought Ryan may have been on to something when he told me he had an off feeling about him, because now I saw what he meant.

After hours of long-winded company meetings, it was finally time to pack up for the evening. I wasn't making any plans tonight at all. I just wanted to curl up on my couch with my feet up.

"Have a good night Ms. Quinn," Karen said on the way out the door.

"So, Sheila—"

"Don't," I interrupted. "I'm going home tonight."

"Okay, well I'll see you tomorrow then," John responded.

"Harsh, much?" Ryan interrupted.

"Listen, I have something really import to do tonight and I don't need *any* distractions."

"Okay, okay. Chill, Sheila. Have a good night."

I grabbed some Indian take out from Rabib's restaurant and drove home. I sat my food down on the coffee table and went into my room to change into a pair of sweats and a tank top.

I pulled a folder out of my safe and brought it into the living room with me. It was Kieran's living will. My Dad had made us all make one once we turned the age of twenty-one. I'd never looked at them, I'd just placed all the files into my safe.

I scanned the notarized document and as I read down to the bottom of the page, there I was, labeled as his power of attorney. So, if he was ever incapacitated, I could make the logical decision to keep him alive or end his suffering. It was scary seeing it in print.

As I took a bite out of my roti, I knew what had to be done. No more denying the inevitable. As I went to close the folder, a small piece of paper slipped out.

For Sheila:

Sis, I know I've been nothing
but trouble for you, but if something
ever happens to me, I know you'll
make the right choice. It'll be tough
I'm sure, but I know neither Shannon
nor Dad can handle it. You'll be
the only one who thinks of me and
not yourself.

Love you Eila,

   -kieran.

He was right. *I took my moment to grieve; now it's time to set you free little bro.*

THIRTY-THREE

I watched as the doctor unhooked the tubes from the ventilator, the machine that gave my family false hope, that made us believe there was a slim chance he could come back even though he never truly could. He was officially gone.

Dad said his goodbyes, then Shannon, and then me. "Rest in peace little bro. I'll never let this break us, but you're in a better place now."

Kieran hadn't had many friends, but a few managed to come to his funeral. As I watched the funeral director lower him into the ground, everyone threw white roses on top of his casket to say their final goodbyes.

It was a rainy and chilly fall afternoon. An abrupt wind blew through the service quite a few times, but we all stayed until his casket was completely covered with dirt.

A harsh reality set in as I walked away from the burial ground: *one day that could be me…*

"Sheila, are you all right? You haven't touched your food at all," Shannon said.

"I'll be fine," I replied.

"Okay, no need to be snippy," she retorted.

"Dad, I know it's our family tradition to have a meal together but I'm just not ready for this right now. May I be excused?"

"Sure, I understand. Call me later."

"Are you serious, Dad? I swear she gets off the hook for everything!" Shannon huffed, rolling her eyes as I left the table.

I felt like something was wrong. I shouldn't have had to bury my little brother that day. He should have still been alive, on the streets doing god knows what. I felt deep down that someone had had something to do with this. Why else would he call me so much that night? Why would he show up on my stairs battered and bruised, barely clinging to life? *I swear if someone did this to him purposely there will be hell to pay.*

I drove back to the office to try and get my mind off it all. It was almost time to shut down for the evening but I didn't care. I just wanted to get Kieran off my mind for a little while.

"Sheila, what are you doing here?" John asked with a suspicious look on his face.

"I just needed to get back here and take care of some things."

"Oh, I see. Well I've, uh, gotta go. I'll see you tomorrow."

I could tell John was hiding something, so I walked over to him, moved him out of the way, and there she was, sitting directly in the front of the conference room. "What the fuck is *she* doing here?"

"Oh, don't look so upset, Sheila. I heard about your brother and came to give my condolences. Then this cute gentleman here introduced himself to me and I decided to hang around for a while. There's no harm in that now is there?"

"There is a lot of fucking harm. If Roger isn't here, *you* shouldn't be here. Now get the hell out of my building!" Ashley Vaughn looked at me with a smug smirk on her face. Flipping her long blonde locks back over her shoulder, she stared at me with her blue eyes, trying to intimidate me.

"And what if I don't want to?"

"Then I'll beat your— "

"Whoa, Sheila, calm down. I'll escort Ms. Vaughn out and you can go back to your office. I think there has been enough drama for one evening!" John yelled.

"Whatever, I better never see you in here again!"

"Holy shit, that's Ashley? She's hot," Ryan whispered behind me. If looks could kill, Ryan would have certainly fallen to his death that instant.

Ashley brushed up against me as she exited the room with John. "Something doesn't seem right about that meeting. I've been here for months and have never seen her come here before, so why would she suddenly show up now all of a sudden?" Ryan questioned.

"I have no idea. She claimed to be here to give me her *condolences* for Kieran's death, but I don't buy that shit for one second. She's up to something, she always is…"

"So enough about her, what exactly are you doing back here?"

"I don't know."

"It must be hard to be around them right now, isn't it? I totally understand. When my uncle Steve died back in Montana, things got real weird among my other family members."

I pushed past Ryan and went directly into my office, locking the door behind me. I pulled the cord to close the blinds, so no one could look in or out. I sat down in my chair behind the desk and spun it around to stare out the window.

I'll figure this out soon little brother. Your death with not be in vain, I can promise you that.

THIRTY-FOUR

I woke up to my phone buzzing violently on my nightstand. I picked it up and the office phone number was flashing on my screen. "Hello?"

"Sheila! You've got to get here quickly, we have a huge problem."

"Okay, John. I'll be there soon."

I looked at the time and it was nine a.m. I never over slept when I had work the next day. *Guess my body had other plans today.*

I rushed into the office to find John waiting by my desk. "What's going on John?"

"We were hacked."

"What do you mean?"

"The blueprints and everything I had have been tampered with." He showed me his laptop and the screen he had with the Nat-Co graphics was all wonky looking and had black marks crossed over it. I still had no idea what I was looking at, but by his expression I could tell it wasn't good.

"Okay, well can it be fixed?"

"Hopefully. I just hope another oil company isn't responsible for this."

What John said didn't make any sense at all. No one knew we were developing an app, so how could another company be responsible for this? I did have enemies, but even they wouldn't be dumb enough to try and tamper with my business, not like that.

"Okay, well go back to your office and handle it, I'll be here if you need me."

"Thank you. I know you don't really understand this coding jargon but I wanted to let you know how serious this could potentially be if your company info fell into the wrong hands."

"I appreciate that, John."

John grabbed his things and headed back to his office and Frank walked right in. "Seriously? What now?"

"I just wanted to confirm your appointment with the electric company."

"Yes, I'm still going. It's this afternoon right?"

"At three p.m. Would you like me to accompany you?"

"I guess I don't have a choice now do I?"

"Thank you for coming today Ms. Quinn. You don't have to say another word, we've already decided to proceed with the merger. I just wanted to see you and tell you face to face. Frank was great—excellent even—at explaining all the benefits to us. He even told us about a few possible hiccups, but I'm sure we'll be able to get through anything. Both of our companies represent strong work ethics and together we can bring in a lot of money."

"Thank you Mr. Kraztski. I appreciate you telling me in person. I'll have Frank contact you once we have all of the contracts drawn up. Have a good night," I replied.

Frank smiled at me with a bit of a chip on his shoulder. "I knew I had them eating out of the palm of my hand, but I wanted you to see how good I was."

"You did a great job, but don't let that get to your head. We'll see how *good* you really are once the contracts are signed and you're in charge of this whole operation."

THIRTY-FIVE

Jacob, the contractor, called the next morning to reassure me that the construction job would be completed ahead of schedule in four short weeks.

I already had my team in place. Rosa was ready to decorate and host the huge release party for me.

I wanted to rebrand it and let Shannon be in charge of it. I wanted it to serve the same purpose as before, but with a twist. The events that used to be held there were more formal and I knew my sister would give it a more modern and upbeat touch. After everything that had gone on recently with our dad being in the hospital and our brother dying, she needed something to occupy her time.

"Sheila, you wanted to see me? You *never* call me—*ever*," she spat at me.

"I know, but I wanted you to know something."

"And what is that?"

"Remember that old Bernstein building?"

"That old event planning place across the street? I saw someone took it over and rebuilt it. What about it?"

"It's yours." With a disheveled look on her face, I watched as the tears welled up in her green eyes.

"Wait…why would you do that? What's the catch?"

"The only 'catch' is that you run that building and you'd better take care of it. Don't let it go to shit. I have enough on my plate, designing and parties is your thing. It'll be the new number one spot to have a function. Watch."

She ran her fingers over her cheeks wiping her tears away. I didn't get along with Shannon, but I figured we could try to since we were the only siblings left. "Thank you," she said as she grabbed her things and left.

"Is…everything okay?" Ryan questioned.

"Yeah, why?"

"Well, your sister was just in here and she actually left with a smile on her face. Oh and there was no yelling or a need to call the cops to split y'all apart."

"I know. She's all I have now and I wanted to try and change the hostility between us."

"Wow, that's a noble thing to do."

"Shut it Smith, I don't have to be nice to you though."

"L-let me grab you a fresh cup of coffee," he said, rushing out of my doorway.

That's what I thought.

It was foggy, damp, and cool out, but I decided to take an early lunch and visit my newest property. I grabbed my umbrella, raincoat, and rain boots from my closet before heading out the door. I told Ryan to forward anything important or urgent to my phone and I'd check it as soon as I could.

A few blocks later, I reached the exterior of the two-story brick building. It looked strong, like nothing could penetrate or destroy it.

I placed my hand on the knob and opened the metal door to start my observation. I wanted this place to have a familiar, but updated look, and that'd better be what I got.

The first floor was completely finished. The entranceway had smooth hardwood floors with several tables where the mock displays would sit. There were four spacious offices filled with plush carpeting, two on each side of the room. I continued my walk down the wooden floor and took the stairs to the second floor. There was going to be an elevator but it wasn't finished yet.

The second floor looked bigger than the first. There were ladders and buckets of paint lying around on top of tarps, so I didn't proceed any further. Everything seemed to be coming right along and I couldn't wait to see the finished project in a few weeks.

I went back down the stairs and raised my umbrella to face the rain I could hear pelting off the roof. As I walked down the wet sidewalk I saw Skylar's Boutique and Rose Garden. I decided to go in and place an order for the flower arrangements. It was the last thing I had on my to-do list before I handed everything over to Shannon.

"Sheila, what are you doing here?" Liam asked.

"I've come to place an order for my release launch."

"Oh yeah? When and where is it?"

"In a few weeks, and it'll be held at the old Bernstein place." He cocked his head to the side and gave me a half smile.

"Wow, well that's great! Just fill out this form and we'll handle the rest."

"Thanks." I grabbed the clipboard from him and filled out the short questionnaire. "My event coordinator Rosa will be in touch before the event to make sure everything is up to par."

"Okay. Sheila, what are your plans for tonight?"

"I don't have any."

"Maybe we could go and grab some dinner?"

"Sure, pick me up at seven."

"It's a date!" he yelled at my back as I walked out the boutique's front door. I walked a few more blocks and went into a local coffee shop. The cold from outside was starting to settle in my bones and I needed something to warm me up fast.

"Next!" the cashier yelled.

"I'll have a caramel cinnamon latte please."

"Coming right up, beautiful," he replied. He looked like he'd just graduated high school and that job was going to foot the bill for college. He had long golden locks and his brown eyes had a slight innocence behind them.

"Thank you," I said, pulling out my credit card.

"It's on the house. What's your name by the way?"

"Why?"

"I need to write it on your drink."

"Oh, it's Sheila. Thanks."

I stepped to the side, in front of the pickup window, and waited for my order to be completed. The place was packed and several baristas were working simultaneously and in almost perfect sync with each other to get the orders out as fast as they could.

Soon my name was called and I took a seat in the back of the restaurant near a small window. Most of the people there were college kids glued to their laptops and typing away with headphones plugged into their ears.

I took a sip of the hot coffee and immediately felt the warmth consume my body. I watched as people rushed down the busy sidewalk to their destinations.

"Excuse me, is this seat taken?" a raspy voiced interrupted my window gaze.

"No," I said, pointing to the empty seat in front of me.

"Thanks," the young man said.

I wasn't in the mood for much small talk so I got up and took my latte with me. On my way back into the building, I got a text from Ryan.

Ryan: Sheila, have you checked the company expenses lately?

Me: I'll be up in a few minutes.

Ryan was waiting for me at the front door of the office and followed me back into mine. "What's going on, Ryan?"

"Well, I was filing some of the paperwork that you left for me and noticed a bank statement mixed in. There was 2,000 dollars missing from the account."

"What? Can you bring me the statement?" Ryan quickly bolted across the hall to grab the paper and brought it back to me.

"See? I highlighted it at the bottom."

Ryan was right. I hadn't checked the account in a few days because I'd never had money just up and disappear like that before.

"Where the hell could it have gone? I haven't purchased anything recently."

"Do you think the company could be a victim of identity theft? Or something?"

"I'm not sure. A few days ago, John mentioned something about being hacked. Maybe the hacker that ruined his app also got our bank info too?"

"It's possible. Would you like me to go and get him?"

"No, I'll handle it. Thank you for your keen observation. I don't like people messing with my money."

"Hey John… how are things?" I said, walking into his office.

"Good, I guess. What about you?" he nervously replied.

"Well, I was good until I discovered two grand missing from the company account."

"Whoa, I'm sorry to hear that. Do you have any idea what happened to it?"

"I don't have any leads yet, but I wanted to ask you something."

"Sure, shoot."

"Remember how you told me we were hacked a while back?"

"Yes, what about it?"

"Well, do you think it's possible that the hacker may have gotten access to our company's personal information? Such as names and the main bank account?"

"It's a high possibility, but I doubt it."

"I see. Then do you have any other ideas how the money mysteriously disappeared out of my account? Because I'm absolutely stumped." I had a feeling deep down that John knew what was going on, but I thought he was too afraid to tell me for some reason. I had every intention of finding out what had happened to the money and he'd better not have had anything to do with it.

I stormed out of his office without speaking another word to him. I felt the urge to pull up more bank statements and check them in front of his face, because there was something fishy definitely going on.

THIRTY-SIX

Liam showed up at my door looking as handsome as ever. He was wearing a tailored all black tux and had styled his unruly hair into a controlled mess. He almost looked more like his old self. "Can I come in Sheila?"

"Yes, of course," I said, breaking my gaze. "I'll be ready in a few minutes, have a seat."

I'd just finished applying my makeup and curling my hair before he arrived, but I was still sporting my pink bathrobe. I walked into my bedroom closet and pulled out my favorite suede knee-high boots and grabbed my black and blue sweater dress that stopped mid thigh.

I sprayed myself with Japanese blossom perfume and met Liam in the living room. "Sheila, you look—just—"

"Just what, Liam?"

"Exquisite. Beautiful. I don't think there are enough words in the English dictionary to describe how gorgeous you look at this very moment."

"Thank you," I smiled, flattered that I rendered him almost speechless. "So where are we going tonight?"

"To Porterhouse Steak and Rib Eyes."

It was one of the top steak houses in the entire state. I'd only been there one other time and if I remembered correctly, it was very expensive. "Liam, you know you don't have to try and impress me with expensive dinners, right?"

"I know, but if *you* remember correctly, that was where we had our first *official* date."

He was right. It was the first place we went after he received his first check from the investment company. Memories flashed back in my mind like it had happened yesterday.

He'd had on his father's cheap three-piece suit, trying to impress me, but it looked terrible on him. The suit was three sizes too big and a hideous shade of turquoise. It was the suit his dad had worn when he took his mom on for their first date, so it meant a lot to him.

We arrived at the upscale restaurant and there was a line flowing out of the door and down the stairs. "Don't worry," he reassured me. "I made reservations."

We walked through the crowd of people through the door and right to the hostess station. "Castle, party of two."

The hostess ran her finger down the list and stopped right over his name. "Let me double check and make sure there's a free table." She disappeared behind a black curtain and promptly returned with two menus in her hands. "Right this way Mr. and Mrs. Castle."

"It's Quinn!" I firmly corrected her.

"My apologies, right this way," she said, narrowing her eyes at me.

We were seated in a booth not too far from the kitchen. The smell of grilled steak wafted through the air, causing my stomach to grumble. There was a gold antique chandelier dangling above the table. The table itself was a dark cherry wood and the marble floor underneath it hardly had any signs of wear and tear on it.

Mr. and Mrs. Castle kept replaying in my head every time I laid my eyes on him. No matter how much he seemed to change, I still couldn't imagine being married to him. In fact I felt quite queasy just thinking about it.

The waitress came over to greet us and took our drink and meal order upon arrival. Her name was Trish and she was a polite young girl.

Dinner with Liam became awkward. Neither of us really said much, which was completely the opposite of our first time there. "Liam, what's the real reason you chose here? Of all places?"

His gaze became intense as he nervously ran his palms over the edge of the table. "To be honest, I thought coming here would bring back those lost memories, you know? That spark we once had. I still feel something for you, I never stopped. But being here, now? I'm realizing this was a *huge* mistake."

"I wouldn't call it a 'mistake' per se, we're still getting a nice meal out of it. That's a plus, right?"

"Right," he laughed.

Sheila, bring it up, right now. You need to find out the truth about that night. "Liam, I need to know something."

"Sure, shoot. I'll be totally honest."

"What were you doing in the garage that night? The night I was attacked?" His facial expression changed from happy to spooked in a matter of seconds.

"I-I..." He paused. "I was coming from an event nearby and had parked my car there so I could get free parking. I had no idea you would even be there that night. I heard a loud scream and saw that asshole hurting you and I fucking lost it. You passed out before I could free his grasp from around your neck, but I want you to know I unleashed holy hell on his ass. I thought I was going to get arrested too, after the cops and paramedics arrived."

"So what *did* happen when they showed up?"

"They took him off to jail after stitching and bandaging his face. I gave them my statement, telling them everything I saw. I didn't tell them I knew you or anything. Sheila, I won't lie to you, I thought he killed you and that ate me up inside."

I could feel the genuine concern he had for me. "Why didn't you leave a name or a note for me?"

"I left the flowers and knew you'd figured it out and talk to me about it whenever you were ready. I didn't want to push it."

"I see. Well I appreciate it," I said, reaching my hand over the table, rubbing the top of his hand.

The waitress briefly interrupted with our meals. Liam had a sizzling steak fajita melt with cheese and I'd ordered a surf and turf: sirloin steak served with buttered lobster tails.

"I have a surprise for you. I want you to wear this blindfold until we get there."

I didn't like being surprised like that, but I was pretty curious to see what he had up his sleeve.

A short drive later, he opened my door and led me out of the car. "Let me lead and no peeking!"

He led me down some sort of path and up a few stairs. I sat down on some sort of cushion and could feel warmth coming from behind me. "You can look now," he said.

I removed the blindfold and what I discovered was beautiful. He had brought me to a fancy terrace. There was a fire pit in the middle, surrounded by a stream of water and rocks. A row of cushioned seats surrounded the entire thing with a support beam in all four corners. The top was an abundance of handmade beams evenly spaced apart, allowing the moonlight to peak through.

He handed me flowers he had stored underneath one of the seats and pulled out a basket. "Liam, I don't know what to say."

"Don't say anything, Sheila. I did this for you, for *us*. I needed you to know that I'd give you anything, all of me." He opened a bottle of champagne and poured two glasses. "To new beginnings."

I quickly inhaled the drink, realizing Liam has lost his damn mind. There was no 'us' and this act of kindness was becoming a bit much for me.

"Take me home, Liam."

"Why? We just got here?"

"Liam, take me the fuck home this instant!"

I slammed Liam's car door shut and tried to run up the stairs to my condo as fast as I could. "Sheila, wait!"

"What?" I huffed, trying to ram my key in the door.

He followed me inside and stopped me dead in my tracks. "What is with you?"

"Liam, I can't do this anymore. I appreciate you saving my life and everything, but this is just too much. You deserve a woman who can appreciate you and embrace how much you've changed. Unfortunately for you, it won't be me. Please let yourself out. This 'us'," I said with air quotes, "is over and I don't want to see you again!"

Confused and hurt, he nodded his head in understanding and let himself out.

That was a lot easier than I thought it'd be.

I walked into my bedroom, eying myself in my floor length mirror, and decided my night wasn't over yet. I needed something exciting, or thrilling, to make this night truly epic…but what?

I caught a glimpse of my laptop behind me and it occurred to me. *Bingo!*

"Justin, right?"

"Yes. You're twice as gorgeous in person."

"Thanks," I said, re-crossing my legs on the bar stool.

Justin didn't know it yet, but I knew all about him and his wealthy family. I knew I should feel like shit about cutting Liam out of my life, but it was for his own good. The shit he'd done to me had caused me to numb myself and hide my feelings. *Sure I'm human and I have a fucking pulse, but that chapter of my life is over.*

"So, Sheila, why is a pretty thing like you still single? Any man in his right state of mind would have snatched you off the market by now."

"I guess that's my problem: I haven't found a man in his right state of mind...yet," I flirted, seductively taking a sip from my straw.

Several hours later, Justin and I closed the bar. I wasn't in the mood to screw him but he had something I wanted and I needed to keep him in my back pocket, for safe keeping.

Rumor had it that his father was building a machine that would be able to extract oil from deposits underground with a seventy percent recovery rate and I wanted to be a part of that. If I could get my hands on that technology, Quinn National would be the number one oil provider in the northeast, maybe the country.

"I had a great time," I said, slipping my number into the front pocket of his sports coat.

"I'll definitely be in touch," he smiled.

Justin was very attractive. Six feet tall at minimum, brown disheveled hair, strong chiseled jaw with a dimple in the middle, and the softest amber colored eyes I'd ever seen. He wore a black fedora with a black sports coat and pair of dark wash jeans. He seemed pretty low key for a guy bred into millions.

Something about him intrigued me and I was going to get everything I wanted from him. I could feel it deep down in my core.

"Have a good night, Sheila." His voice was low and husky as he spoke.

"Goodnight."

We both disappeared into our vehicles and went our separate ways.

THIRTY-SEVEN

I woke up refreshed and ready to start my day. I felt like a huge weight had been lifted off my shoulders and happiness in the form of money was coming in place of it. Making money was the number one thing that made me happy, and I'd do anything I could to keep it flowing into my business.

I arrived to work an hour early to get a head start on my day, only to find a note on my office window, warning me to watch my back. I didn't recognize the handwriting and I honestly didn't care who'd left it because they hadn't had the balls to say it to my face.

I ripped the note off my door and tossed it directly into the shredder. I placed my coat on the rack and tossed my brief case on my desk, quickly joining it and taking a seat at my desk. I booted my computer and heard Ryan come in as I waited for it to load.

"I'll bring you a cup of coffee in a few minutes, Ms. Quinn."

"Take your time, Ryan. Nothing can fuck up this day for me. Absolutely *nothing.*"

"I wouldn't say 'nothing' Sheila."

Ryan left and quickly returned with a fresh cup of coffee and a manila folder with a red letter S stamped on the front of it. That S stood for one thing and it was the worst thing you could think of: someone was trying to sue the company. There was only one way I could get out of this and it was paying my old friend, Judge Henry Johanson, a visit.

After two painful hours of staring at the fine print, I came up with a plan. Those greedy assholes weren't going to earn a cent from this company.

"Judge Johanson, I'm so glad you were able to meet with me on such short notice."

"You said it was an urgent matter, Ms. Quinn. I made sure to free my schedule for the next two hours *just* for you."

"I won't need more than one hour, sir," I flirted, handing him the manila folder. I walked around his large masculine desk and rubbed his shoulders while he pulled his reading glasses out of the front pocket of his striped shirt.

Judge Johanson was a very compassionate and understanding man. He also wasn't bad looking for a fifty-something –year- old man. He looked a lot like Burt Reynolds, but carrying an extra twenty pounds.

"Sheila, do you know if they signed a waiver by any chance?"

"I believe so, and to my knowledge they were both already granted workers' comp."

"How long did it take them to be seen in the hospital?"

"One victim went right away, the other hesitated."

"Bingo. I can get this case dropped before it is even leaked out of this office for you."

"Thank you so much! What can I do to repay you?"

Judge Johanson was very easy to manipulate, and he was also a sleazebag. I blew him off before I left and that's all it took to confirm the whole nightmare would disappear.

I returned to the office with a huge smile on my face. Sure, I'd had to blow the most powerful attorney in the judicial system, but I'd also gotten what I wanted—as usual.

"So…how'd it go?" Ryan questioned.

"Let's just say, those greedy bastards just *blew* their chances."

"That's awesome! You really have the magic touch, Ms. Quinn."

"More than you know," I smiled, running my finger over my bottom lip.

"Have you been able to pin point the source of the missing money yet?" Ryan asked with a stern look on his face, changing the subject.

"Not yet, but I'm sure I'll find out. I *always* find out."

Lately, Ryan had been trying to keep tabs on me and I didn't understand or appreciate his demeanor. If I told him I was leaving the building, he'd never questioned me before, he'd just let me go and tell me to be careful. Now I felt like I had my dad breathing down my neck all over again.

I barged into Ryan's office and slammed the door shut behind me. "What's wrong, Sheila?"

"Why have you been breathing down my neck lately? I share a few vulnerable moments with you and now you feel like you can keep tabs on me?" I glared in his direction with my hands on my hips, impatiently waiting on his response.

"No. It's just... I worry about you. I know how much your brother meant to you and the fact that you haven't taken the time to grieve him concerns me."

I lowered my hands as I processed what he'd said. He was right, but I didn't have time to grieve Kieran; I had a company to focus on. I could take time off later and grieve then. "Well, I don't have time to deal with that right now," I huffed.

"That's your problem right there, Sheila. You shut everything down: your feelings, your compassion, *everything!* No sane person could keep levelheaded with all of this corruption and bullshit around them!" Ryan stood on his feet and walked in front of me, gazing into my eyes. "Sheila, it's okay. You're here with me, you can trust me. You know that right?" he said, calmly rubbing my shoulders.

"I don't know who to trust, *anymore*," I pulled away from his grasp and let myself out of his office.

As much as I hated to admit it, I did need to grieve my brother's death. After work, I drove to Oak Monuments Cemetery with a fresh bundle of flowers to set in front of his headstone.

I ran my hand over the grooved marble and stared at the engraved quote on the front. *Beloved son and adored brother.*

I did adore him, but I was also disappointed in him. We had been so close when we were younger, but the older we became, the more our lives went down two completely different paths; mine was business, and his was drugs.

I kneeled down into the cold dirt and placed the white lilies in front of his stone. "Kieran, I'm so sorry this happened to you. You know I still blame myself for not answering the phone that night. I lost track of what was more important. If I had taken your warning seriously, you might still be here with me." A tear rolled down my cheek and onto the dirt below. I felt a cool chill roll by my neck and knew it was my brother reaching out. "I know. I love you, too."

THIRTY-EIGHT

It was less than a week before the launch of my new event planning business. Shannon and I had been bickering back and forth over a name. I wanted something catchy and she wanted something that represented our relationship—I was pretty sure "Bitch to Bitch" wouldn't be a good business name. Honestly, the name was the least of my concerns; I just wanted her to run an effective business and not fuck me over.

After three excruciating hours, we finally came to a mutual consensus on the name: "Sister to Sister Event Planning". It was catchy and at that point I would have agreed to almost anything just to get her to shut the hell up about it. Everything else was also finalized and prepared to run smoothly.

"Sheila, which dress should I wear?" Shannon yelled from behind the fitting room door.

"I don't know, the pink one I guess," I huffed.

We've been in the Custom Chic Boutique for over an hour and the launch event was later that night. I still hadn't even finalized my own outfit yet.

She finally opened the door and looked like a runway model. Her pink dress was fitted at the hips and flared open in the front from the thigh down. Rhinestones encrusted the bodice and made her look like a million dollar princess. She was glowing from head to toe in it. "That's the one. I have got to go now."

I ran out to the parking lot. I rushed home to dig through my closet and narrowed my choices down to two.

After a nice relaxing bath, I stared at my options on the bed and chose to wear my sheer top with black embroidered flowering over the breasts, paired with a knee length satin skirt that had two rows of ruffles stitched across the front, and my black pumps with a silver flower embellishment on the side.

I pinned my hair back into a nice French roll and applied simple make up to my face before heading out the door.

I pulled up in front of the building and it definitely looked like a red carpet event. The valet opened my door and led me to the sidewalk before parking my car for me. A red carpet was literally stretched from the sidewalk to the front entrance door. There were velvet ropes holding the press and ticket holders back until we officially opened at eight o'clock.

"Ms. Quinn, Ms. Quinn, what inspired you to host this beautiful event at this revamped building?" a news reporter questioned.

"You're going to need to talk to Shannon Quinn. She was the one responsible for breathing life back into this old place."

"Ms. Quinn, Ms. Quinn, you look gorgeous tonight. Are you here alone?"

I glared at the nosey reporter and kept walking to the door. Two huge bouncers in all black uniforms with the word staff etched on the front of their shirts opened the door and escorted me inside.

Purple, white, and black spot lights were swirling around the room and then landed right in the middle of the wooden dance floor where I was standing. "What do you think, sis?"

"I'd tell you if these bright lights weren't blinding me, Christ!"

"Sorry." She turned them off and after my eyes adjusted I was able to look around the place. She'd been able to transform the old office space into an open party zone.

Two long rectangular tables stretched from the wall to the top of the dance floor, draped in purple and white tablecloths with matching centerpieces with onyx stones surrounding the base. She had managed to get two chandeliers placed on each end of the building too. She'd also knocked down the back walls to really open the place up right in front of the elevator. "It's beautiful Shannon."

She ran over to me and pulled me by my arm. "Wait 'til you see upstairs!"

When my sister was in her element, she shined. She was a nice, fun, bubbly person and an actual *pleasure* to be around.

We took the elevator to the second floor and she made me close my eyes until we got there. "Open them."

The second floor was even more gorgeous than the first. The same decorations were in place, but there were mini cooking stations with chairs surrounding them and extra seating in the back. The offices were still intact and decorated to accommodate people. I also saw pamphlets with the company logo printed and scattered everywhere. Scented flowers also decorated the floor, giving it a more elegant feel.

"Open the doors, Francisco!" she shouted through her head set to the bouncer below.

It's show time.

As we arrived back on the first floor a few deliveries were still being made as the guests rushed in, including raw food and flowers.

Shit I hope he didn't decide to personally show up too.

Several hours later, after endless mingling and countless interviews, the event was starting to dwindle down. I went to the bathroom after my last interview to freshen up and take a breather. I applied a fresh coat of lip stick and powdered my face. I heard the door creak open behind me and who I saw behind me was the one person I hadn't wanted to see that night.

"Li—" He ran over to me and grabbed the back of my neck, forcefully pushing his lips against mine, trying to penetrate my mouth with his tongue. He hiked my skirt and sat me on the edge of the sink. He slid my panties to the side and ran his fingers over my clit, then dipped a finger inside. I could feel myself getting wet and hated that he still had that power over my body. He removed his hand from my depths and unbuckled his pants, pumping his cock a few times before he entered me.

There was a fire, a deep intensity in his gray eyes. I felt like he was trying to reclaim me as his.

I grabbed the back of his neck as my pussy tightened around him, grasping every ounce of pleasure from it. A loud moan escaped my lips as my body quivered, begging to release. He slowed down, just as I was giving in, to torture me for a moment longer before regaining his pace. I couldn't hold it back any longer and as he rubbed up against my clit, I lost it. I felt like my body was his puppet and he had control of its strings.

He freed me from his grasp after he came inside of me and tucked himself back in his pants. "I missed you too," he said with a sly grin.

"Liam, listen. You'll always be important to me. I shared some of the best times and the worst times of my life with you, but I just can't do this again. The hell you caused me isn't something I can easily forgive and forget. I need to be alone…all alone."

He grabbed my arm. "Sheila?" He said staring into my eyes deeply, looking for something that was no longer there. "I'm different now, can't you see that? We're both different."

"Exactly," I said as I slid my skirt back down my thighs. "Good bye, Liam."

I met up with Shannon outside and told her I was leaving a little early to head home.

The event had been a huge success and was talked about on every local news station. It was even printed on the front page of competing newspapers.

Shannon texted me in the morning to tell me that she was booked solid for the next two months with new clients and to thank me.

Liam had called me several times later in the night and I was pretty sure he showed up at my place a few times, but I meant what I said. I really couldn't go down that road with him again. The feelings just weren't there, no matter how *hard* he fucked me or *where* he fucked me.

I could still feel the soreness from him, but it didn't change anything. There was only one person I had my sights on now and that was Justin. He had something useful and I needed to do whatever it took to wrap him around my finger to get it.

As I got ready for work, I texted him to meet for dinner around seven tonight. He agreed only if he could choose the place, which was fine with me. *I'll play along with his games for now.*

THIRTY-NINE

After a short drive down the freeway, I pulled into the parking lot of a Mexican bar and grill named Turbana. I had never heard of it before, but I was starving and for some reason, trusted Justin.

I parked my car and saw him waiting by a red Chevy pickup truck in a long black trench coat and leather boots. "Is that your truck?" I asked.

"Why yes it is. I call her Ol' Reliable. Don't get me wrong, I like sports cars too, and I know they're all the rage, but I prefer low profile and will take a classic any day. Anyway, shall we?" he said, bending his elbow to receive mine.

We walked up a flight of stone steps to a small building. It had huge windows reaching from the ceiling to the ground and you could see all the way to the kitchen from the front door, which was nice. It felt more personal. Justin opened the door for me and the smells swirling around the room were wonderful. Waiters and waitresses in red and green uniforms were serving people their food on sizzling hot plates and as soon as I saw the chicken fajita plate, I knew exactly what I wanted.

We were seated in a booth in front of a large brick archway with an orange painted wall underneath. There were paintings of flowers and other Mexicana artwork. The building was made out of mostly bricks with some updated wooden beams stretching across the ceiling with fans mounted over each table.

The waiter, Jose, was very polite and told us about all the house specials on the menu without even looking at it. I was already set on the chicken fajitas so I ordered that immediately and let Justin pick out our drinks. Jose placed our order and came back with a couple of pink lemonades and free chips and salsa to snack on while we waited for our meals.

Justin and I sat in silence, locking eyes as we both reached for the freshly baked chips and salsa. It wasn't weird or awkward; it was actually nice not to be questioned and just eat.

Our waiter and a waitress came out with two sizzling plates and placed them down in front of us. Justin also got fajitas but with steak instead of chicken, and we got a margarita pitcher.

After dinner I invited Justin over to my place, which was something I didn't normally do. I left him on the couch while I grabbed a few drinks from the fridge. "Is Moscato okay?"

"It's perfect," he smiled back at me.

"Cheers!" I said, tapping my glass against his.

"So Justin, tell me more about yourself. You mentioned that your father builds things. What kind of things does he build?"

"Honestly, anything you can imagine, he could find a way to build it, but he's more known for his ROV units."

"Remotely Operated Vehicles, right?"

"Correct. How'd you know about that?" he asked with a puzzled expression on his face.

"I'm a lot smarter than I appear I guess." I grinned before taking another sip of wine.

"What kind of work do you do?" he questioned.

"I've recently taken over my dad's company."

"That's nice. Well look at us, both working for our dads," he laughed. "Hopefully you enjoy your job, though."

"Who wouldn't enjoy bossing others around?"

Justin and I talked all night long. He gave me a shit ton of information about himself and I barely had to spill anything about myself, which was just what I wanted. For once it felt nice to talk to someone and get to know the real them for a change.

The next morning I rushed into the bathroom to shower and get ready for my work day. I had a meeting with a well-known app developing company and wanted to compare them to John. I felt he was taking an awfully long time to develop something that seemed so simple and I was starting to second-guess his true intentions at Quinn National.

"Hi, Mr. Inuyasha. Thank you for meeting with me today. So can you tell me more about your app technology and how fast you could get it up and running?"

"Absolutely, Ms. Quinn. For the service you require it would take my company no longer than two weeks. That includes debugging and thorough testing. We'd have everything on a backup server and in the event your system is hacked or temporarily shut down, our security systems would scramble the data so they couldn't steal any information. Also, our app team can translate English into different languages to suit your clients needs."

Everything this man offered sounded three times as good as the bullshit John was feeding me. He offered extra security and our data couldn't be compromised; John has been working on it for a month with hardly any progress and we'd already been hacked once.

"You're hired. Quick question, your app wouldn't interfere with the other current data development right?"

"No, ours will be on a brand new server, but I strongly suggest getting rid of the other one. If it's not running by now, there's something definitely wrong with it. May I see it by any chance?" he asked.

"I'll find out for you." I went back over to my desk and paged Karen to send John to my office.

"You rang, Ms. Quinn?" John snarled sarcastically.

"Yes. Do you have your app data with you by any chance?"

"It's on my phone," he responded nervously.

"Could you show it to Mr. Inuyasha please?"

"Sure," he said handing his phone over to the short Japanese man with gray hair.

Small beads of sweat formed on John's forehead as Mr. Inuyasha quietly studied the app. I could see the panic starting to set in just by his subtle nervous ticks.

"Thank you," Mr. Inuyasha said, handing him his phone back.

"That'll be all for now John, thank you," I said, dismissing him from my office. Mr. Inuyasha looked at me and shook his head with disapproval. I knew then that John definitely had ulterior motives.

"Thank you for your time, Mr. Inuyasha. I'll definitely be getting rid of the other app developer, and I'll be in touch with you in a few weeks." He shook my hand and left my office. As soon as the door was shut, I texted Lucky.

Me: I need a favor.

Lucky: Anything.

Me: Can you hack into apps?

Lucky: Ha. Is the sky blue? Piece of cake.

Me: Good. I need you to hack into the Nat-Co app here. Something is off about John and his fishy business.

Lucky: You got it. I'll also dig up some dirt on John too while I'm at it.

Me: Thanks. I owe you one.

Lucky: You've done enough. But I do need a favor from you.

Me: What?

Lucky: I'm going to drop off a thumb drive to you. I need you to plug it into John's computer for sixty seconds and then rip it out and leave it at the dog park for me.

Me: Can do.

A small package was delivered to my office and inside was the thumb drive from Lucky. I paged Ryan to my office so he could take John out to lunch and buy me some time to plug it into his computer.

"Yes, Ms. Quinn?"

"Hey Ryan, why don't you grab John and take him to lunch? He barely leaves his office and I think it's time for you guys to get to know each other. Take the company card and enjoy yourselves."

"Okay, but why would I want to get to know him?" he said, arching his eyebrow at me.

"Because he's the new man around here and he'll be playing a very important role in our company, being the new app developer and all," I lied through my teeth.

"Okay, whatever you say!" he answered, staring at me suspiciously. "What's in the box?"

"I have no idea, but I'll find out soon. John's on his way up, so hurry up and get ready to go!"

I watched as John and Ryan shook hands in the hallway and left. I opened my office door and walked to the front office where Karen was, just to make sure they were actually gone. I walked back down the hall and took the stairs one flight below my office to John's.

His office door was unlocked, but I didn't see his computer anywhere. I looked all around his cubicle and before I accepted defeat, I saw that he had left it on the conference table. It was locked, but Lucky told me I would still be able to upload the data and eject the thumb drive without John ever knowing I was near it.

I panicked at every sound I heard around me. It felt like the longest sixty seconds of my life and I was nervous he would be back at any second. I finally saw the green bar pop up on the screen, so I ejected it and tried to leave everything how I'd found it. I went back upstairs to my office and grabbed my jacket to run and meet Lucky at our meeting spot.

I left the box on the table and walked away from it. I stood by a vacant tree and saw Lucky come over, grab it, and walk off. I hoped he would be able to get me some answers.

FORTY

It was almost six o'clock and my weekend was just minutes away. I'd signed every legal document that was piled sky high on my desk, checked and replied to every single email in my inbox, and checked that our stocks were still in the green and in good standings.

I wanted to do something different this weekend. I felt like disappearing for a couple of days to regroup and I knew just the perfect person to do it with.

> *Me: Hey Justin, I'm not sure if you work Fridays or not, but I wanted to know if you have plans for the weekend.*

> *Justin: Nope, I don't work Fridays, but I do need to get away from here. This has been a very stressful week for me.*

> *Me: Any idea where we could escape?*

> *Justin: There's this lake house about thirty minutes away. Meet me there, tonight.*

"Ms. Q, sorry to interrupt."

"Yes, Ryan?"

"I was wondering if you had any plans for this weekend. I thought maybe we could go for a run, maybe go an even longer distance?"

"Sorry Ryan, I've already made plans, but I promise I'll make it up to you. I feel like we haven't spent much time together lately."

"Same here," he said, pouting.

"Come here," I said curling my finger back in my direction. He walked over to my chair behind the desk and I wrapped my hand around the bottom of his tie, yanked him down to my eye level, and planted a kiss on his innocent lips. I could see my kiss affected him in more ways than one when his bulge became quite noticeable through his slacks. "That'll give you something to think about all weekend. I have an idea, but I'll let you know about it in a few weeks. Just try and think warm thoughts."

I closed the office down and went to the garage to retrieve my car. I entered the address Justin had given me into my GPS. I stopped at home for a brief moment to toss some clothes and toiletries into my overnight bag, then got back into my car.

I entered the highway and it was smooth sailing down I95. I flew down the highway, taking in the gorgeous scenery on the side of the road as I drove by.

The exit for Lake O'Gashi was on my right and it was the first time I was actually nervous to meet someone.

Justin was standing in the middle of a wooden dock leaning up against a metal rail when I pulled up. He was so entranced by the warm fall foliage that he didn't even notice I was right beside him. "Hey," I interrupted.

"Hey!" he responded, wrapping his long arm around my body, pulling me closer to his side.

"How long have you been waiting here?"

"Oh, not long at all. I was leaving the office just after we spoke. It's beautiful out here isn't it?" he asked.

"Yes it is," I replied, admiring the view. Most of the leaves on the trees had turned and were full of dark ambers, oranges, and yellows. The reflection of them off the water was breathtaking.

"It's nice to get away from the congested city streets and smog filled air sometimes. I really needed this, Sheila."

"Me, too."

"Are you hungry?"

"I'm starved. I accidently skipped lunch today."

"Good, come with me then," he said, grabbing my hand and leading me down a short leaf covered trail to a small luxury cabin.

"Is this yours?" I asked, scanning every inch of the property with my eyes. The cabin had two floors, with green trim surrounding the windows, roof, and shutters. The wood on the porch was smooth and rounded at the edges with a black bench in front of the window. He unlocked the white front door and inside looked brand new, but he pulled me through so fast I didn't get a chance to look around.

We went straight to the kitchen and there was a picnic basket sitting on top of a hand carved wooden table with two chairs. He pulled out one of the chairs for me and assumed his place on the other side of the table. The table was set with plastic spoons, forks, and paper plates. He opened the basket and pulled out a bottle of red wine, cheese, an assortment of fruit, and some wrapped sandwiches. He split everything equally between us and I couldn't wait to dig in. Everything was perfect and I savored every bite.

"Thank you for this, Justin. I don't remember the last time I had a quiet picnic."

"Me either."

"So Justin, tell me a little bit more about this place. Did you build it?"

"Yes and no. I designed it, but my father's company actually put it together for me. I told you, if you can imagine it, he can build it."

"This looks amazing," I said as I took a moment to take in the actual construction of this place. The kitchen and living area were all in the same space. There was a fireplace and a bear skin rug on the opposite side of the room with a long black couch and television. The kitchen had a hand carved island in front of the all black fridge and the floor was a simple polished wood.

Justin stood up and cleaned the table off and then came back to grab my hand. "I know what you're thinking, everything looks hand carved right?"

"Yes it does."

"Well you're right, it is. My father developed machinery to smooth wood without losing its natural structure."

"Wow," I said as I gazed into his amber eyes.

"So Sheila, how did you know about ROVs?" he said as he led me over to the bear skin rug and retrieved a block of wood for the fireplace.

I decided to be honest with him; I didn't feel like I had to lie about my knowledge of that. "Okay, I know about them because my company has been trying to obtain one for quite some time."

"What kind of company do you run?"

"I work at Quinn National, Justin."

"Wait, the oil company? Wow. My dad told me he's been wanting to do business with your company for years."

"Seriously?"

"Yeah. But I guess your father wasn't easy to convince at the time."

"That sounds about right. Well there's a difference between me and my father. I've done my homework and I'm more than interested in doing business with you. I know that your machinery has a high success rate with underwater extractions."

"You certainly have been doing your homework. I'll tell you what, we'll talk business on Monday, but for now let's just enjoy each other's company."

"Okay, I can deal until then."

He went back into the kitchen and retrieved another bottle of wine out of the fridge, grabbed our glasses, and brought them over to me. He filled the glasses. The fire had grown quite significantly, filling the room with a mild heat and a warm glow.

"Cheers!" we said simultaneously.

"Sheila, there has been something I've wanted to do to you since the moment we met."

"What's that?" I said, placing my glass down beside me.

"Kiss you," he said, wrapping his hands on either side of my face, pulling my lips into his. His gentle but possessive grip sent chills down my spine.

He broke our kiss momentarily to gaze into my eyes. Those amber orbs were gorgeous and full of lust. He was the perfect gentleman. A rare gem, lost in a sea full of assholes, and there he was, giving himself to dysfunctional me.

"Justin, wait."

"What's wrong, Sheila?" he questioned as he leaned in closer to me.

"I…I—don't know."

"Just relax." He gently regained his grip behind my neck and the reflection of the fire behind us made his eyes sparkle.

Slowly lowering me back onto the soft rug, he kissed me once more, raising my arms above my head and interlocking his fingers with mine. He sat back on his heels above my pelvis and lifted my shirt from my stomach and over my head with my help. Running his hands over my stomach then around the arch of my back to unclasp my bra, I felt the heat rise from in between my legs.

He ran his smooth hand over one breast and pulled the other into his mouth. As he twirled, pinched, and sucked my nipples, I could feel the heat ignite throughout my entire body.

As his hand left my nipple and traveled down my navel to my mound, he lifted the silk material and rubbed my clit through my lace panties. Soon his mouth traveled the same path. He tugged the skirt from my hips, and my panties soon followed.

With my legs spread wide, he positioned himself on his stomach in front of me. He dipped a finger inside of me, before locking his jaw on my clit.

Licking, sucking, and twirling his tongue around my pussy, he drove my body wild. I started shaking uncontrollably from the intense pleasure he was giving me and reached down to grab a hold of his head as he continued feasting on my private parts.

He sucked and twirled his tongue once more in one quick motion and I lost total control of my body, intensely convulsing as he held my legs down and locked his jaw again until I saturated the rug below.

He ran his fingers across his mouth, wiping away my essence as he grabbed a condom wrapper out of his back pocket. He stood to his feet and dropped his pants and boxers right in front of me, revealing his nice cut legs and large cock.

He rolled the plastic over it and kneeled down in front of me, pulling my hips toward him. Rubbing the base of his cock against my opening, he teased me before slowly entering my body, stretching my walls as far as he could without hurting me.

Justin made love to me by the fire. It was just us. I felt like he was giving me pieces of his heart that I didn't deserve.

We'd only physically met a few weeks ago, but I'd known about him for quite some time, so being there in that moment, completely vulnerable with him, felt right.

There was a spare room attached to the den on the opposite side of the living room and that's where I awoke the next morning. The rays of sunlight peered through the windows, temporarily blinding me as my eyes adjusted to the brightness.

I ran my hand over the empty spot next to me and realized Justin was gone. He'd left a silk robe on the chair beside me and I quickly slipped it on then followed the sweet aroma drifting through the air.

"Good morning, sleepy head," Justin said, placing a mug of fresh coffee on the counter before turning his attention back to the stove behind him.

"Morning. What are you making?"

"It's an old family recipe for cinnamon crepes with a sweet cream glaze and fresh strawberries."

"It smells amazing," I said, grabbing the coffee mug from the counter. A sweet vanilla scent rose from the frothy mug and I realized he had made me a homemade espresso. This guy was definitely a charmer, but I had to keep my newly developed feelings for him under wraps.

Justin and I fucked, admired the scenery, and got to know so much about each other in the short three-day getaway. Unfortunately it eventually came to an end. We both had to leave and get ready to keep running our companies the next day.

"Justin, I had a great time. I'm glad you invited me out here."

"I did too and I hope to do it again sometime in the near future. It's even more breathtaking during the winter months," he said, squeezing me in between his arms. I inhaled his dry musk scent and wished I could get one more round of fucking in with him, although my entire body was still sore from the last round.

"I'll be in touch," I said, heading toward my car.

"I'll fax you the paperwork in the morning so we can this merger going."

"Thanks," I smiled as I closed the door and started the ignition.

You're mine now Mr. Fitzgerald.

FORTY-ONE

I had my legal team look at the paperwork Justin faxed over the next morning to make sure it was legit and confirm that he wasn't trying to fuck me over.

Mr. Inuyasha sent me an email later in the morning, updating me on the app he was developing. He told me it was coming along nicely and should be completed within the next week.

"So, how was your weekend? You look refreshed," Ryan said with a hint of sarcasm in his tone.

"I'm quite refreshed, actually. Glad you noticed."

"I notice a lot about you."

"So how did the lunch date with John go the other day?" I asked, changing the subject.

"Good. Turns out he's not a complete ass face."

"Good. I'm glad you guys could bond."

"Whoa, I didn't say we did all of that. The dude was okay, but he did admit that he had the hots for you."

"Aw, did that make you jealous?"

"No. I had the hots for you first." He smiled as he went back across the hall into his office.

I decided to go downstairs and pay Mr. Keegan a visit to see if he'd made any more progress on his shitty 'app'.

As I approached his office, I overheard him talking about me. "She's hot, but she really needs to lighten up. She always seems like she has a dick shoved up her ass," he laughed.

"John, you're absolutely right, I should lighten up," I interrupted.

"See, I told you," he said, nudging Frank. "Not to be disrespectful, Ms. Quinn, but ever since your brother died, you've been kind of a bitch."

I politely smiled at him and nodded. Little did he know, me being a bitch was in my nature, but he was going to find out the hard way how big of a bitch I could really be.

After a long day at work, I grabbed some Indian take out before finally arriving at my condo. Lucky had messaged me before I left the office wanting to meet me urgently, so I had him meet me at my place. I could tell by the tone of his voice that he'd found out something big.

"Thanks for meeting me here, Lucky. What were you able to find out?"

"Sheila, you may want to sit down for this."

"Why?"

"Because," he sighed, taking in a deep breath, "what I'm about to tell you is really going to send you over the edge."

There it was again, that feeling in the pit of my stomach, only this time, it felt much worse. I sat down on my couch and prepared for the worst. He sat down beside me and pulled his laptop out of his bag, turning it around on his lap so I could see the screen. The pictures I saw on the screen froze me in place. There was a picture of John and Keith—together and shaking hands.

"Sheila, do you know these two men?"

"Yes. John Keegan and Keith Lee, what about them?"

"Did you know that they were both con artists?"

"No I didn't. What kind of con artists are they?"

"From what I've discovered, they've scammed hundreds of businesses out of money and real estate. They infiltrate your company, find something you really want, and once they know they can black ball you, they try to convince you that you *need* their help and watch you fail miserably. If that doesn't work, they offer you some shitty app service attached with spyware to collect more personal data from you."

"Are you fucking serious?"

"Unfortunately. Have you done any business with Keith at all?"

"You could say that. He was trying to take my permit for the property across the street. He wanted to take me out on a date and fuck me in some dirty hotel in order for me to keep it."

"And I'm guessing he wasn't successful, so he sent John in to save the day."

"Now I know why that asshole was so eager to meet with me again: he knew his friend was already in. But I don't understand. Keith showed up at my job first, how would he have gotten information about me if I hadn't met John yet?"

"I have no clue, Sheila. I did find out something else though and you're not going to like it."

"What is it?"

"They're brothers and they both have a lot of information on you and your family Sheila. Seems like they've had their eyes on you for quite some time."

Lucky showed me a slide show full of pictures he had found of Shannon, Dad, Kieran, and myself from the thumb drive I gave him. None of us were ever pictured together, just out and about separately, which was odd. It was like they were personally stalking each of us, like some sick creepy type of paparazzi. The last picture he showed me almost caused me to punch the wall behind us. Someone had taken a photo of Keith with my brother in an alley, on the same night Kieran was trying to call me. He must have known something was up.

"That son of a bitch! They've fucked with the wrong woman. They took my brother from me and now they're trying to take my company? These assholes will *never* know what hit them!"

"Sheila, whatever you need, you know I'll take care of it. Kieran was my best friend, even though we lost touch."

"I know. I'll be in contact soon," I said, giving him a kiss on the cheek.

I shut the door behind Lucky and could feel the rage building, deep down inside of me. I wanted to find John and Keith and kill them both myself, but I knew it was too risky. I knew as the CEO of a huge company that I'd run into people trying to manipulate me, take advantage, and hell, even try to seduce me. But to get my family involved and get one of them killed? That called for an act of revenge, and I would get mine.

"Thank you for inviting me over to your place, John."

"No problem," he said, licking his lips as he stared at my voluptuous breasts bursting out of the top of my skin-tight, revealing dress.

He slid beside me on the couch and starting kissing the side of my neck. "Wait, John, before we do this, could you get us something to drink?"

"Sure, I'll be right back."

I removed my coat and placed my purse down on the floor beside me. "Here you go, I'm going to run to the bathroom," he said, placing his cup down beside mine. "Don't move!"

As I waited for him to come back, I took a sip of the wine he'd placed on the table in front of me.

"Back, now where were we?"

"We never said cheers, and that's awfully rude."

"Sorry," he said tapping his glass against mine then swallowing a huge gulp of the bubbly liquid.

He ran his hand over my cheek, pushing my hair behind my ear. Then he traced his lips from my ear down to my collar bone, sending chills down my spine. "Sheila, I don't feel right."

"What's wrong?" I said pulling his bottom lip into my mouth with my teeth.

"I—don't—know."

"Maybe you should lie down and let me take over."

He lay back on the couch and I unbuttoned his shirt, revealing his toned tight abs and hairless chest. I kissed his lips and ran a trail of kisses all the way down to the bulge in his pants. I unzipped his pants and slid the head of his cock into my mouth. "You sure have a beautiful cock, John. Too bad this will be the last time anyone is near it ever again, you son of a bitch!"

"What do you mean?" he said, trying to move but couldn't.

"You fucked with the wrong family. I know that you and Keith are brothers and were working with Ashley Vaughn to try and fuck me over."

"What are you talking about?"

"It was no coincidence that you found me in the bar that night. You were following me. And your brother gave my druggy brother his final hit before he ended up in the hospital. Now I know why he was calling me so much: he knew I was in danger."

His eyes were starting to glaze over and his speech was becoming inaudible. "What's the matter John? Cat got your tongue?"

I grabbed his cheek and slapped the shit out of it, then I texted Lucky the address so he could come over and take care of the problem for me.

I watched John closely as he tried to mouth words, but no sound was coming out. It gave me great pleasure watching him suffer like this, just like I was sure he got pleasure knowing my brother suffered.

There was a light knock on the door and I looked out the peephole before opening it, just in case it wasn't Lucky. "Thanks for getting here so quickly, he's nice and sedated for you," I said, placing one last kiss on John's lips before I let Lucky take over.

"Thanks." I watched as Lucky pulled a black case out of his bag that was full of syringes.

"Hello, John, my name is Lucky and I'll be taking care of you tonight." I watched as Lucky stuck him in the leg with one of the syringes and John's pupils dilated. He seemed to be more alert and focused, but he still couldn't move or say anything.

"What did you give him?"

"A special concoction I made. It keeps them alert, but still has a high dose of sedative so they can't move. I want him to know what I'm doing even though he won't feel it…at least not at first…"

John's eyes widened when he fully comprehended what Lucky had said. Lucky pulled out another case full of scalpels and other medical equipment with a look of pure joy on his face.

I stood by the door and watched as Lucky removed John's pants and sliced thin pieces of skin off of his leg and placed them in a plastic bag. John didn't move at all, but the fear was written all over his face. I felt completely numb inside watching the dismemberment.

"I'm going to go now, make sure you clean up this mess. I don't want it linked back to me, Lucky."

"Will do, Ms. Quinn."

I'd do whatever it took to keep my family and business safe. I'd lost my brother due to my own negligence and I would never forget it. Keith Lee was going to learn the hard way that he had fucked with the wrong woman. I would *personally* make sure he *never* forgot the bullshit he put my family through. *I lost my brother and now he will too.*

FORTY-TWO

The day of John's funeral, I had to pretend to show sympathy for his family and mourn the loss of the employee that had tried to fuck me over. I dug deep inside myself to find a time where I'd experienced nothing but sadness, and that was when my mom died. I felt the heat from my tears sting my eyes and knew it was game time.

Keith was bawling his eyes out reading his brother's eulogy. He looked so pathetic and I wished I could have killed him too, but watching him suffer was much more fulfilling.

The service and burial were short and sweet and as the preacher finished his speech, I tossed a flower on John's casket as they lowered it into the ground and left. I called Ryan to ask if he was ready for our trip and he didn't answer, which was strange.

I rushed home to change out of my drab black pant suit and into something more fun: a black see-through lace top and some capris. I needed to get away from this world and go somewhere where there would be lots of sun and less death and paperwork.

I'd booked a trip for Ryan and me to the Virgin Islands. As my limo arrived in front of my condo, I tossed my bags on the porch and the driver retrieved them.

I gave myself a final onceover before I locked up my apartment and tried to call Ryan again. He didn't answer, but the limo was headed to his place next.

The driver honked the horn twice after two more failed phone calls. Finally, the door popped open and Ryan didn't seem quite like himself. He wouldn't let the driver take his things and appeared to be upset and on edge. He let himself into the car after dumping his bags in the trunk and told the driver to piss off.

"Ryan, are you all right?"

"Yeah, just a sad day, I'm ready to get drunk on the beach and forget all about it."

We arrived at Logan airport and had to catch a short flight to New York City for our connecting flight straight to the Virgin Islands.

Seven hours later, we arrived on the white sandy beaches of Saint Thomas. The water was crystal clear, the high was ninety degrees, and, unlike Massachusetts, the air smelled fresh. We hailed a cab and drove a short ways to our hotel.

Our driver grabbed our bags and an assistant from the hotel came out to greet us and grab the rest of our belongings. We were escorted through huge white doors into a colossal lobby with a metal chandelier and a tan colored marble floor. I could feel the cool breeze blowing through the side entrance from the pool as we walked by. We approached a huge stained wooden desk and gave the attendant our information. Then two different assistants escorted us to our room on the second floor.

The assistants left our luggage by the side of the massive king size bed and told us to enjoy our stay. Ryan and I were close behind and I was astonished at the sight, barely able to take it all in at once. The instant urge to explore struck me.

The bathroom was behind us and it was the cleanest bathroom I'd ever laid my eyes on. A his and hers double sink was mounted on top of a granite counter top and dark cherry cabinets. The shower had a glass door with brand new beige tile and was big enough for two people inside. A separate whirlpool bath tub was right beside it with water jets attached. The same tan marble that was in the lobby also decorated our hotel room floor.

The bed was neatly made and draped in white linen with a green throw blanket and pillow sitting on top of it. A double door was on the opposite side of the bed and I quickly ran over to open it. I discovered a vast balcony with two lounge chairs and a glass table in between them. We had the perfect view of the crystal clear water, sand, and coconut trees. I felt like I was in heaven.

Ryan plopped down on the bed, disturbing my mood by complaining that he was tired, but I wanted to look around. I grabbed my keycard and my purse and went downstairs to find a bar.

The bartender gave me a piña colada in a medium sized coconut with a cute pink umbrella and a glass of wine. They were both on the house because he thought I was the most gorgeous thing he'd ever seen. I inhaled the colada before I went outside and took the glass of wine with me to explore.

I carried my wine around as I checked out the pool, dance club, and a few restaurants to potentially have dinner at that night. Everyone was so laid back and friendly, much different from my life back at home. It seemed like a true paradise.

I found a cozy spot outside on a nice red lounge chair and placed my drink on the table. I kicked my feet back and reminisced about the insane life I had. I raised my glass in the air and said a quick cheers aloud. "Cheers to you, asshole, for thinking you were clever enough to take this company from me. This is my empire, and no one in this life or death will fucking change that."

I relaxed my head back after taking a sip and felt my phone vibrate in my purse with a text from Lucky.

Lucky: Hey are you busy?

Me: Yes I just started my vacation.

Lucky: Well, we need to talk NOW!

Me: Call.

"Sheila, I did some more snooping around and found some startling information. John and Keith had a third brother, a half brother to be exact. He didn't move here until a few months ago though."

"Okay, so?" I huffed. "He told me he had two brothers and a sister."

"Well, apparently he is also a part of their con jobs. He's usually the first one to infiltrate. Since he appears younger, he applies to businesses as an *intern*."

"Lucky, stop fucking with me! What did you find?"

"His name is Ryan, Sheila. Ryan Smith…"

I dropped my cell phone on the table for a moment when Lucky revealed the name to me. A cold chill traveled down my spine and I was speechless, unable to process the horrible truth that I was now faced with. I placed the phone back up by my ear and managed to muster, "I, um, are you sure?"

"Sheila, I'll text you a picture of the three of them together."

I checked the message and it was in fact Ryan. He looked different; his hair was a lot lighter, but otherwise he looked the same.

"Ryan is here with me on vacation. Do you think he knows? He's been acting weird since we left the state."

"He might. I'll be on the next flight out, be careful."

I gulped my wine and ran back upstairs to my room to see if Ryan was still there. He wasn't on the bed but his stuff remained. The bathroom door was closed and I heard the sound of the shower going. *Shit, what do I do? What if he knows I had a hand in his brother's death?*

I sat down on the bed and heard the door open. "Hey, I didn't hear you come in. Are you all right? You look spooked, like you've just seen a ghost or something."

"I'm all right, are you okay? You seemed kind of down earlier."

"Yeah, just have a lot going on right now. Family matters, but don't let it dampen your mood. I hope you found us a place to eat on your journey."

"I did. I think I'll go freshen up so we can go and grab a bite to eat."

I took my bag in the bathroom with me and ran the fan, hoping the foggy mirror would clear up. I didn't have that weird feeling in the pit of my stomach, but I still felt uneasy about being in the same room as him.

Ryan and I had dinner at a surprisingly quiet bistro. As I ate my chicken parmesan, I couldn't take my eyes off of him. Lucky texted me and told me his flight was delayed, but he'd be here as soon as he could. When he did arrive, he promised not to interfere unless he had to, but he'd watch from the shadows and keep a close eye out for me.

"Sheila, I'm stuffed. Maybe we can take a bottle of wine back up to our room and spend the rest of the night there," Ryan said.

"Sounds good." I managed to slip one of the steak knives in my purse when he briefly left for the bathroom, just as a safety precaution. We couldn't take weapons on the plane and I didn't want to be defenseless in the event things went haywire in our hotel room.

Ryan grabbed my hand and led me back to our hotel room. I could feel the alcohol I'd inhaled consume my body, making me feel drunker than usual, and horny.

Once inside, Ryan pushed me against the wall and traced his warm lips on the side of my neck. He pinned my arms back at my sides and continued his assault on my neck, then over my shoulder.

My phone violently buzzed inside my purse snapping me out of the sexual trance I was in. "I need to check that."

"Go for it, I'm going to hit the little boy's room."

I grabbed my purse off the floor and looked at my screen.

Lucky: Sheila, he knows! I hacked his email and found this.

FWD: KILL HER.

RYAN,

SHE HAD HIM KILLED. OUR BROTHER TEXTED ME THE NIGHT SHE WAS THERE AND FELT SOMETHING WASN'T RIGHT AND THEN I FOUND HIM DEAD. I KNOW THAT WASN'T A COINCIDENCE. I KNOW YOU'RE GOING ON VACATION WITH THAT BITCH, BUT I NEED A LITTLE MORE TIME TO DRAIN HER COMPANY'S BANK ACCOUNT. ONCE I GIVE YOU THE SIGNAL, KILL HER. I DON'T CARE HOW CLOSE YOU PRETENDED TO BE WITH THAT SELFISH BITCH, BUT SHE DESERVES TO PAY FOR WHAT SHE DID TO OUR BROTHER.

-KEITH

Me: What do I do?

Lucky: Just act natural, if he snaps I'll be right next door. Make sure you're armed just in case though.

Me: Will do.

I placed my phone on the nightstand and sat on the edge of the bed, carefully sliding the steak knife out of my purse and placing it under his pillow for safe keeping. I pulled my shirt down off my shoulder to let him know that I still wanted to have sex with him.

I heard the door creak and the sound of his voice traveling from the short hall startled me. He walked over to me, now in the nude, and gently pushed me back on the bed. He grabbed the material of my shirt completely off my shoulders, sliding it off my body and onto the floor. "Sheila, I miss this. I miss what we had before things got so crazy."

"What do you mean by that?" I questioned.

"You just got so wrapped up in everyone else around you, it seemed like you forgot about the only one who has been there for you these past couple of months—me."

"Ry—" He silenced me with a passionate kiss, igniting a deep fire within me that missed his familiar touch.

He ran his cool hands over my lace bra, feeling my warm breasts underneath. I lifted my torso off the bed so he could unhook it, freeing them. He ran his tongue over my breast bone then gently twisted the dark bud in between his fingers before pulling it into his mouth.

A soft moan escaped my lips as he tortured me with his tongue and fingers on both breasts simultaneously. His warm mouth traveled down my navel and over my mound. My body was wet and ready for him to take what he wanted. He ran his fingers over my capris, removing them, then felt the lace, rubbing the top of my clit. Yanking the fabric from my hips, he spread my legs wide, inhaling my scent.

He flicked his tongue over my clit and dipped a finger inside of me, rubbing the most sensitive part of me. He spread my folds then buried his face in them, licking and sucking on me until my body trembled with pleasure. "Sheila, let me do this for you, just this once."

I didn't understand what he meant until he grabbed the base of his raw cock, pumped it, and slid it inside of me. My pussy gripped him tightly as he forced his way inside of my slick opening. He gazed at me with his deep blue eyes, making me experience a different kind of pleasure in the art of making love.

He raised my arms above my head, keeping himself balanced as his strokes picked up the pace, until the room was filled with the sound of our wetness slapping around and the smell of our essence. I could feel my core tighten, wanting to release, but I held back, trying to fight the urge. "Sheila, you never held back before, don't start now."

The cool husk of his voice was enough to send me over the edge as my body succumbed to the pleasure. He slammed into me harder, rubbing against my sensitive clit and causing my body to spasm and come again. His body tensed as he rammed into me once more before his warmth filled my insides.

His body was still intertwined with mine as he said the unspeakable. "I'm sorry it has to end this way, Sheila. I really didn't want to hurt you, but I had to feel you one last time." He grabbed my pillow and stuffed it over my face, trying to squeeze all of the air out of me. I frantically kicked and in a last ditch effort, I slid my hand underneath his pillow and pulled out the knife I'd hid. I stabbed him in the chest and twisted it, feeling his arms release me from my suffocation chamber. I pushed him onto the floor and watched his color fade as he reached for the metal piercing his heart.

I kneeled down on the floor in front of him, rotating the knife once more to make sure he would bleed out. "Nothing personal Ryan, but you should know by now that you do not *cross* the boss!"

ABOUT THE AUTHOR

Niquel is the author of The Forbidden Series, The Teacher's Pet Series, and her newest project, The CEO will be out this spring. Boston born and raised, she's attended two colleges for 3D Animation and Graphic Design. She's been independently published for over a year now and has no intention on slowing down anytime soon. When she's not busy entertaining her two daughters and supportive significant other, you can find her sipping her double cup of coffee, writing, or chatting with friends online.

Niquel loves to meet new fans and she'd love to hear feedback from you. Whether it's positive or negative, your reviews help her grow as an author! You can contact her directly through any of the sites posted below.

www.facebook.com/author.niquel

www.twitter.com/authorniquel

www.authorniquel.com

Authorniquel@aol.com

www.goodreads.com/authorniquel

Other Works by Niquel:

A Forbidden Love

An Endless Love

The Teacher's Pet (A full novella coming soon)

A NOTE FROM THE AUTHOR

If you've made it this far, thank you! I hope you've enjoyed this crazy character I've created! I wanted to create a world where women were in control for once, and weren't ashamed to dominate men and take what they wanted. I hope I proved myself worthy of your time. Thanks and don't forget to leave a review!

Feel free to join The CEO discussion group on Facebook! https://www.facebook.com/groups/800819660004614/